Preface

In my early years, my family was members of the Presbyterian Church. As I grew up, we moved from my hometown to a nearby rural area; as a consequence of this move we began visiting in this rural area 1 specific Methodist Church that was founded in the mid-1800s. During my college years, I was introduced to the Church & I was baptized into Christ in early 1983.

I first began reading the Scriptures as a boy not always understanding what I was reading, but always curious about what the Bible had to say. Early in life, I learned of the concepts of holy beings versus unholy beings, good versus evil, & God versus Satan. While evil does exist in the world, we make choices that sometimes have unintended consequences & and we may very well be culpable either when things go badly, or innocent people are harmed. Throughout my spiritual journey, I have been cognizant of Satan & the influence that he has on this world.

This book is by no means a tribute to Satan or his followers. At the end of the day, it is a novel that conveys a number of *fictional stories* concerning Satan's influence on the world. The inspiration for this book stems from two similar experiences separated both by distance & time. The awful sound of something that sounded neither like an animal or a human; a low-pitched growling sound from deep within the growler's lungs. The first occurrence when I was just a boy in the Deep South happened as my brother & I returned from a walk on our land; upon hearing the awful growling, both of us ran as fast we could back to our house. The second occurrence was in September of 2013 in

North Carolina as my wife (then fiancé) & I walked one evening near her apartment complex. We were sitting on a bench near the sidewalk when we both heard the growling sound. She turned to me & said "I am scared. We need to leave now."

My wife is from a different part of the world & practices a different faith than I. We both love God, but we both are convinced that the enemies of believers are Satan and his followers. With that being said, this book is not a religious or spiritual book as a commentary on the Scriptures. It will contain graphic language and violence that is a realistic portrayal of the world in which we live. YOU HAVE BEEN WARNED; if this is not your style of book, please stop reading now…

Otherwise, join me as I put to paper my ideas & thoughts on Satan & his influence on our world.

Chapter 1
In the Beginning

Long ago, when both the heavens & the angels were created, all was right between God & his angels as we loved & worshiped Him. God loved us as a father loves his children. We were loyal to Him & were eager to please Him. We thought that it would always be this way; that we were objects of His affection & the apples of His eye. Everything seemed perfect to us & we loved Him with all our being. Angels were created sinless & disobedience to God was simply not allowed.

Little did we know that God had in His mind the concept of creating humans; beings that are inferior to angels in every way. Yet, God seemed to turn his affections away from us & focused His attention on humans. Some of us felt that God had betrayed us & that He no longer cared for us. We could not understand how He could love such weak & pathetic creatures more than us. Some of the angels were obedient to God & did not want to challenge His will.

We soon learned that we would not only be called upon to be messengers for these humans but would also protect them in certain situations. We could not believe it. Serve humans that were below us? Some of us became incensed with anger, but we did not dare voice our displeasure until we could not take it anymore. Soon, there were whispers of a revolution for our celestial rage. It was during this time that I, Lucifer – The Bearer of Light, began to hate humans. As a result, I & like-minded angels attempted a coup & we were utterly defeated. Once we were defeated, we were banished from Heaven

& the only home we had ever known. My

honorable name of Lucifer – The Bearer of Light

had been stripped of me & my name was changed to

Satan.

My judgment, my punishment for defying

God will come soon enough. Unlike humans, we

have no forgiveness – no way to atone for what we

tried to do. It is said that misery loves company, so

now I will take as many humans with me as

possible; that is probably the only pain that I can

inflict back on God for casting us out of Heaven.

My demons & I take special pleasure in causing the

innocent to stumble – especially the ones that seem

so pious & devoted to God. We consider it a two-

for-one – we hurt God & we hurt the ones that

stumble. We have studied humans since the

Creation. We understand their strengths &

weaknesses in order to exploit their weaknesses &

make them fall from God's grace. We use every human weakness against them: addiction, anger, desire, division, gluttony, greed, hate, jealousy, lust, pride, shame, etc. - you name it, we use it.

Let me be crystal clear – we hate ALL humans regardless of culture, gender, national origin or skin color; we are equal-opportunity haters. We do not care about which Scripture or religion that you claim to practice. We do not care either what economic or governmental system you employ. We do not care about your beliefs or customs. All we care about is creating a division between humans & God. We know that the time of our death, destruction & judgment are near – we are running out of time. We are then working as hastily as we can to bring forth chaos & carnage to every corner of this world. If we can cause you not only to stumble but to lose faith & convince you that God will not save you, the deception is all the sweeter

for us. I have no qualms in crushing all of you – my

eternal sworn enemies.

Therefore, you no longer must ask why bad

things must happen. Life is not fair - or – as some

humans have said "Life is a bitch & then you die."

Anything we can do to make you stumble, we will

do. The greatest ally that we have is the belief that

we do not exist & the denial that we may have

caused someone misfortune. Now, as a human, you

know what you are up against. Haters going to hate.

Let the games begin & I will see you soon...

Chapter 2
The Fatal Five

Briar paced nervously as he waited for the demons to deliver the names of their next targets. Even though he had been promoted, he wrestled with trusting the demons – knowing that they could destroy him in the blink of an eye. A part of him loved seducing innocent virgins and draining their life energy, but another part of him sees his victims' faces in his sleep & still feels a tinge of guilt & shame over his victims' demise & eventual deaths.

The demons appeared to Briar on the Linn Cove Viaduct along the Blue Ridge Parkway in Western North Carolina at midnight. A winter storm had forced Park officials to close the section until the road was cleared of ice & snow – so no one had witnessed their rendezvous.

Mangum, his demon superior, grabbed Briar by the neck & shouted "Pathetic human! Why do you want to be one of us? Do you not know how good life on Earth is? Do you not know that we would trade places with you if we could?"

Briar grabbed the hand of the demon and flung it away from his neck. "Mangum, you do not know the difficulties of being a human! You do not know what I have been through, how every woman I ever knew growing up let me down and betrayed me. For every innocent virgin that I seduce, I get back a little of my self-respect."

"Foolish human. Satan does not care about your suffering or your supposed self-redemption. He wants lost souls and if you are not able to deliver them, he will strip you of your demonic powers and you will go back to be a normal human," exclaimed Mangum. "There are other

Incubi that are more than capable of replacing you in the Fatal Five!"

"My apologies Mangum!" cried Briar.

"You are to go to Lynchburg, Virginia to the Christian college there and you will be shown the virgins to seduce. The girls-only residence is in the South Tower building. Make your way there and we will show you your targets. You know what to do from there," replied Mangum. "Collect the 4 succubi & take them with you to Lynchburg; they will also have quotas to meet there." The next morning, Briar headed out to meet the others in Valle Crucis...

"Fuck! I don't want to leave Valle Crucis! I love this cabin and the river. Why can't we just stay here?" exclaimed Rose.

"Rose quit your whining. You sound like a little punk ass bitch," replied Lily.

"Rose don't sweat it. We may come back here sometime," added Holly. "Lily, you need to cut Rose some slack. You were the same way not that long ago," continued Holly.

"Okay succubi sisters, we need to get out of this jacuzzi in 15 minutes & get packed to leave. Briar will be back soon, and we will probably have to leave for our next assignments," said Ivy.

"I hope I get a strong, athletic type this time – with mesmerizing eyes, a beautiful smile and a big fat penis," added Rose. "I want him to ride me hard!"

"We get who we get – unless we catch a boy by surprise," replied Lily. "We have to take the bad with the good. Besides, if you get one that you fall for, you will have a harder time when he dies."

"You sound like you know from personal experience," said Rose.

Lily was unable to dry her eyes while she tried to get Jonathan, the man of her dreams, out of her mind. "We can't have loved the way a normal woman can… If we try, everyone we love dies & we are left alone," As the tears came back, Lily found herself inconsolable, angry & sad. "It's not fucking fair! What good is it to have all this power & at the end of the day, we are alone & lonely!?!" She climbed out of the jacuzzi & without another word grabbed her towel & after drying off went back inside the cabin to shower off & then pack.

Holly, Ivy, and Rose climbed out of the jacuzzi, dried off & went inside the cabin to shower off & pack. Just as Holly, Ivy, Lily, and Rose finished packing, Briar arrived to pick them up.

"Hey Briar," exclaimed Ivy. "So, where are we headed now?" she asked.

"Mangum says we have to go to Lynchburg, Virginia to a Christian college & he will give us further instructions," answered Briar.

"Holly, why do we have to listen to what Mangum says?" asked Rose.

"Because Mangum is in charge of us & is ultimately responsible for what we can accomplish," replied Briar. "Besides, none of us are strong enough to challenge his authority. If he appears before you Rose, be humble, don't look him in the eye, and be quiet. You don't want to anger him – you won't survive what he would do to you."

"The SUV is unlocked so you ladies need to take your stuff & load it in the back," added Briar. "Holly, it is your turn to ride shotgun upfront with me."

"I don't mind if I do!" exclaimed Holly & winked at Briar. She liked to practice her seduction skills on Briar – knowing if she could make him lose control, then what normal man could resist her advances?

"Holly! You are such a thot!" cried Ivy – mildly jealous that she was not practicing on Briar.

"Ivy, you are a bigger slut than I will ever be!" replied Holly.

"True that! I do love men & I can never get enough," answered Ivy. "Sometimes, I want the entire football team to run through me like the Holland Tunnel! I love to feel all tingly inside!"

"Damn girl – you got it bad!" said Rose.

"Ivy, we talked about this… no unbridled lust with a large group of humans," replied Briar. "There would be too many casualties at one time & we would bring too much attention to ourselves."

"Oh Briar! A girl can dream, can't she?" insisted Ivy.

"Just so you understand," continued Briar.

Ivy interrupted Briar "Yea, yea, yea, I fucking get it! Can we go now dammit?" Ivy was steamed and got quiet in her anger.

After all their belongings were loaded, Briar cranked the SUV & they made their way from the cabin back down to the main road. Their GPS directed them to travel north towards northwestern North Carolina into Tennessee and eventually into Virginia to pick up Interstate 81 North. As they made their way onto Interstate 81 North, Holly started stroking Briar's crotch.

Briar pulled back her hand & said "Holly, don't start what you can't finish. If I lose it, are you going to catch it? We don't need my seed all inside the car."

"I will not only catch it, but I will also get rid of it!" replied Holly.

As Ivy, Lily, and Rose slept in the backseat, Holly again started stroking Briar's crotch. After he started getting harder, she unzipped his pants & started stroking his penis. Holly then bent over & started fellating Briar's penis long & slow. Briar tried to keep control of the car but found it more difficult the more Holly went down on him. Just as he came with his penis in Holly's mouth, a herd of elk came over the embankment – causing Briar to swerve to miss the massive animals. Briar lost control of the SUV – which was now descending a mountain ravine. The SUV crashed through tree limbs & branches – slowing down their descent but ripped off the doors of the car.

Lily was thrown from the car & woke up falling through the air – screaming at the top of her lungs. She was able to break her fall with tree branches, but both her back and her left arm were killing her. As she lost consciousness from the pain, a dark specter picked her up & flew back to his castle. She would provide his meal for the night or so he thought…

Ivy and Rose were disoriented after the crash – murmuring to themselves…

"What happened?" asked Ivy.

Holly laughed a sinister laugh & said "Well, I made Briar lose control in more ways than one!"

"You're sick Holly!" exclaimed Ivy.

"That's messed up," added Rose.

Briar walked up & wiped the blood from his temple. "Where in the hell is the car?"

Mangum & his demons appeared out of the mist. "We replaced it. Briar, if you can't keep your succubi in control, then perhaps we should replace you too. Go across the river and go around the bend of the dirt road; there you will find your replaced car and your effects. Try not to crash this one. Follow the dirt road to the end & you will access I-81 from there."

Holly timidly approached Mangum and said "Master, I am sorry for causing this delay."

"FOOLISH HUMAN! YOUR STUPIDITY ALMOST CAUSED THIS WRECK – SO YOU ARE NOT TO PLEASURE ANOTHER WHILE HE IS DRIVING," yelled Mangum as he glared at Holly. "Lucky for you that the elk stampede caused the wreck and not your foolish games."

"Briar, it appears that you are missing one of your succubi. Find her before you continue your journey; otherwise, we will have to permanently replace her," continued Mangum.

"We will search for her immediately," replied Briar. Mangum and his demons disappeared in an instant.

By the time that they notice Lily was missing, the vampire had already taken her to his castle in the mountains of West Virginia – far away from them.

They all started calling out for her. "Lily! We need to go! Lily! Where are you?"

"We need to fan out and try to find her. Meet back here in an hour. If we don't find her, then we have to bring in a replacement," said Briar.

"Are we so worthless to you? So easily replaceable?" cried Rose.

"You heard what Mangum said. It has nothing to do with the value we place on each other. It has to do with serving Satan in completing our assignments – or someone else will," replied Briar.

"Rose, you search east. Holly, you search south. Ivy, you search west. I will search north," continued Briar.

François, a vampire, placed Lily in the bed of his master suite which was nestled away in the north tower of his castle. François' castle was located between Rich Mountain, Harper Knob, and Little Middle Mountain, West Virginia. Lily remained in a coma from the accident trauma. She had a cut near her left temple that had stopped bleeding, but she had dried blood down the side of her face, neck, and shoulder. The left side of her blouse also had dried blood on both the left shoulder and upper chest.

"Master, did you bite her carelessly and spill some of her blood?" asked Jean Luc, one of François' human servants.

"No," replied François. "She survived a car accident, but she is in a coma. I was going to feed on her but sensed that she is different."

At that moment, Celeste, a human housemaid was coming down the corridor.

"Celeste, we have a guest in the master suite who has survived an accident. Please treat her wounds and tend to her needs should she awaken from the coma," requested François.

"Certainly Master. I will tend to her at once," answered Celeste.

"Different in what way Master?" inquired Jean Luc.

"She may not be completely human or not human at all," answered François. "Her body temperature is much warmer than most humans. Her hair and her skin also smell different. Her eyes have a slight red tint which I saw before she went into a coma. She is not snoring but is making a strange sound – almost like a growling sound."

"Master, how does she smell?" questioned Jean Luc.

"Old – she smells very old," replied François.

"Like you Master?" continued Jean Luc.

"In some ways perhaps, but not entirely like me," answered François. "I have seen a creature like her before & I believe that she may be a succubus, however, it is hard to tell until I speak with her & see how she behaves while awake. Jean Luc, there is something else – she was not traveling alone. She was traveling with a male & 3 other females. For this reason, they may be the Fatal Five. Out of all the incubi & succubi created, these are the deadliest – the most lethal to other humans. Through their seduction skills, they can mesmerize both the most innocent & the most defiled humans according to not only the object of their desires but also their absolute lust for power. Their goal is to be fully transformed into demons through their ability to offer human souls to the devil.

"If they are indeed the Fatal Five, they may be able to eventually track her down here. Beginning in the morning when I retire for the day, double the guards outside the castle, alert all security staff, and ensure security protocols are strictly followed. We cannot take any chances. Individually, they cannot overtake me, but perhaps together they could overwhelm me.

"I will try to reach her while I sleep & she sleeps in the coma. Perhaps I can get the answers that I seek," said François.

"Master, I will inform the entire security staff immediately and we will be vigilant both night and day," replied Jean Luc. "We will ensure the castle is secure at all times."

After François retired to his coffin for the day, he focused solely on his new guest to connect with her through telekinesis. *"I am François, the Master of this castle and your host. I am mystified by you and wish to learn more of you,"* thought François. *"Centuries ago, I was a normal human in the Montreal, Canada area, but one night I was seduced by a beautiful vampire and was turned a short time later. For years, I gorged on as many victims as possible every night. Then, everything about being a vampire became disgusting to me. After moving to these West Virginia mountains, I found a peaceful, quiet existence and now feed just enough to pacify this vampire virus."*

Lily was not yet able to reply through telekinesis although she understood François' thoughts. She became aware that her body was in a coma, but her mind was now awakened. Lily wondered to herself if perhaps François may be immune to her powers and that she may be immune to François' vampire virus. For the first time in centuries, Lily began to have a glimmer of hope; while the circumstances would not be ideal, they would be a vast improvement over her current circumstances.

While she enjoyed sex with virgin boys, she would invariably fall in love with them – only to feel their life-force enter her and leave them. She watched with pity the former virgin boys slowly die a cruel death. Her deep-seated anger & rage stemmed from not being able to have what she really wanted. She often wondered if the whole succubus existence was worth it – for at the end of the day all Lily wanted was lasting love. While the presence of her succubi sisters and her incubus brother were a source of both companionship and support, she had felt for a quite a while that her heart was no longer into being a succubus. Could it be that a relationship with François proves to be mutually beneficial? This possibility helped Lily release some of the anger and rage that had crippled her from connecting with others and her surroundings.

Suddenly, she felt her mind open & she placed her sole focus on François and began to channel all her thoughts to François. *"I am Lily and all that you told your servant Jean Luc is true. I am a succubus and a member of the Fatal Five, but ready for a change, ready to have a home, and ready to have someone to call my own. My family left Europe in the 1680s because of insane witch hunts & we relocated to the New World to live a peaceful life. Our tranquility in the area now known*

as Danvers, Massachusetts was short-lived for the

Salem Witch Trials began in 1692. By the time they

ended, my parents, sister and best friend had all

been executed – murdered by superstitious,

ignorant, & religious fanatics. In time, the

Commonwealth of Massachusetts paid reparations

to those of us surviving family members.

"Initially, I became a succubus to exact

revenge on the religious fanatics for murdering

both my family and my dear friend. No amount of

reparations quenched the intense fury that I felt for

the locals. I seduced as many of the boys & young

men as I could – draining their life forces at a

frantic pace; so much so, that many of the guilty

individuals left Massachusetts. After I had punished

the families responsible for the murders of my loved

ones, my fury subsided but has never completely left me. Even now, I struggle to control my temper."

"Lily, it is understandable how you came to be a succubus & I do not judge you in the least. May I offer you a possible explanation of why you struggle to control your temper? I cannot say for certain, but I do wonder if you never grieved the loss of your loved ones. You are still trying to reconcile the horrific tragedy that befell them & you replay those events in your mind – reconsidering all the possible actions that you could have done to save them. Because of this reiteration of events, you may also feel recondite guilt that at times overwhelm your emotions. It seems to me that you may want to return to Massachusetts someday to visit the final resting places of both your family and your friend. There may be conversations to be had that are long overdue. With that, I will leave your

mind in peace & I will allow you to consider these suggestions," thought François.

Lily relaxed her mind & drifted off into a deep, restful sleep. While Lily slept, Celeste entered her chamber to treat her wounds & was able to slip off Lily's blood-stained top & remaining clothing. She was trying to determine the extent of Lily's injuries & to launder Lily's clothes. After treating Lily's wounds, she at once sent Lily's clothes to be laundered. Lily's body was completely covered by the bed linens, but Celeste wanted to keep watch over Lily until her cleaned clothes could be placed back onto Lily before she awakened. Once Lily's clothes had been returned to her chamber Celeste slowly & gently placed the garments back onto Lily & covered Lily once again with the bed linens. Celeste then turned at once & left Lily's chamber closing the door – locking it as she exited the chamber.

Celeste had already requested a guard posted outside Lily's chamber door. When she saw him, she exclaimed "No one but me & Master our allowed to enter this room! Please advise us should she wake up & want to leave her room."

"As you wish Celeste," replied the guard.

"Did any of you see any sign of Lily?" asked Briar.

"I did not find anything – no shred of clothing, no strands of hair, no blood & no scent of her," answered Ivy.

"Ditto," replied both Holly & Rose.

"Damn! It's as if she vanished," exclaimed Briar. "We better continue on to

Lynchburg. We will hit it hard & perhaps Lily will meet up with us there."

"I don't think so. I think Lily is gone forever. I think she wanted out and will use this opportunity to move on from us," asserted Ivy. "Although she loves sex, she was sick & tired of the lifestyle. She was wanting to stop moving & settle down somewhere."

"If that is true, then Mangum will assign her replacement to us," replied Briar. "Once we are back on I-81, keep watch for someone trying to hitch a ride with us."

As the group made their way near Lodi, Virginia they spotted a young woman near the next exit trying to flag them down. Briar exited it off the interstate and unlocked the car door. The young woman was hesitant to open the door – so Briar rolled down the window.

"What is your name?" asked Briar.

"Mangum sent me," replied the stranger.

"WHAT IS YOUR NAME?" yelled Briar.

The stranger looked both ways and back at the group.

"We don't have all day! Either tell us your name & get in the car or we will leave your ass on the side of the road!" roared Briar.

"Mangum gave me 4 names to remember & strict instructions not to enter the car unless I was certain of your identities. My apologies, but I must know your names," answered the stranger.

"I am Briar. They are Holly, Ivy, & Rose," said Briar.

"Those are the 4 names that Mangum gave me. I am Iris," replied the stranger. "Mangum briefed me on our Lynchburg mission." Iris opened a car door, sat down in the car seat, & buckled her seat belt.

"Briefed you on our mission? Damn Iris, you sound like military!" exclaimed Holly.

"Former military. I am a Marine & also did a stint in CIA – assisting in breaking child sex rings," answered Iris.

"Awesome Iris! You got to tell us more!" said Holly. "Wait! How did you become a succubus?"

"Holly, that is a story for another time," said Iris. "Let's just take care of business in Lynchburg for now."

"Iris, I admire your focus," said Briar.

"Compliments of the Marines and the CIA," replied Iris.

Later that evening, Lily woke from her coma – in pain from the car accident, but otherwise okay. As she looked around her room, she had an immediate appreciation of her host trying to make her as both comfortable & welcome as possible. As she pulled back the bed linens, she was surprised to see that her clothes were clean. She went to her suite door, but when she tried to open it she discovered that it was locked from the outside in the hallway & she began to knock on the suite door.

"Hello? Is anybody there? Hello? Please let me out!" said Lily. Lily continued to knock until someone replied. Suddenly, she heard the door unlock & open. Celeste stepped through the door & introduced herself.

"Hello, my name is Celeste. I am François' most senior housemaid. I will take you to see him at once!" exclaimed Celeste.

"I am Lily. Before I go anywhere else, I seriously need to use the ladies' room," replied Lily.

"Lily, you have your own personal ladies' room in the corner of your suite. You even have your own fireplace inside the bathroom," stated Celeste.

"Thanks Celeste. I will be right back," answered Lily.

Moments later, Lily returned & Celeste took her to François' library – which was open & spacious to be less intimidating for Lily's introduction to François.

"Wait here Lily. I will inform the Master that you have awakened," stated Celeste.

After a short time, a side door of the library opened & François emerged. "Lily, please allow me to introduce myself – I am François, the Master of this castle."

"Hello François. Thank you for your kind hospitality. Your castle is beautiful," answered Lily. "I have seriously contemplated your advice & I do believe it would be beneficial to visit my ancestors' final resting place in Massachusetts."

"Excellent Lily!" I will take you after you have had dinner – you must be famished," said François.

"Celeste, please have the kitchen staff to prepare a fine meal for Lily. In the meantime, I will give Lily a tour of the castle," added François.

"For obvious reasons, the curtains are drawn during the daylight hours if I wake up before sundown," continued François. "Other than that, feel free to move around the castle as you please."

After Lily had a chance to eat her first meal in days, François took Lily in his arms & flew to the Danvers, Massachusetts area. After some time, she remembered the precise final resting place of her ancestors. For the sake of privacy, François distanced himself from Lily giving her time & space to address her ancestors. Overcome with both grief & shame, Lily fell to her knees with her head bowed, crying hysterically from her broken spirit & shattered heart. She tried to speak but was paralyzed with sadness & heartache.

A gentle wind blew & Lily began to hear the voices of her ancestors.

"Lily, you have avenged our murders & you have not forgotten us, but you have let rage and bitterness consume you for much too long," exclaimed her ancestors. Looking up, Lily saw the spirits of her parents, her sister, and her best friend.

"You have let your blind hatred lead you astray & you have victimized the innocent. You must turn from your evil succubus ways & return to the values that we passed down to you. We love you & look forward with hope to the time that we can be together again," continued her ancestors.

Lily began to feel the hostility & rage leave her being – realizing all the wrong that she had done.

"Loved ones, please forgive me for the wrong that I have done & for the shame I have brought to our family," cried Lily. "Down through the ages I have missed you all so much & have filled the massive void of your absences with the wrong things. I will spend the remainder of my life honoring your memory & the values that you have instilled in me."

"Someday, we will see you on the other side. We love you Lily & farewell for now," replied her ancestors.

"Please don't go," begged Lily.

"We have stayed as long as we are allowed. Goodbye dear Lily," replied her ancestors.

"I love you all too. Goodbye for now," said Lily. Lily saw the spirits of her loved ones fade from view.

Lily suddenly felt dizzy & her head was spinning. Her blood pressure bottomed out & she lost consciousness, but François caught Lily in his arms. She remained unconscious until the next morning where she woke up in bed back in her suite of François' castle.

François was right. For the first time in forever ago, Lily felt like her old self from her years growing up in Europe before everything changed & they were forced to move to New World. The rage, bitterness, & hostility that she felt for so long were gone. It was replaced with calm, inner peace, & tranquility. She now had a sense of purpose &

renewed hope. Her days of being a succubus were over; she had François to thank for that fact. She would now dedicate the rest of her life to helping François any way that she could – including helping him find a cure for the vampire virus.

The Fatal Five continued east on I-81 until they took I-77 South before picking up Virginia Highway 58 in the Hillsville, Virginia vicinity. The GPS still showed over 90 miles to Danville & it was getting late into the night, Briar decided to check them into a hotel while they were still in Hillsville.

"We will just have to go the rest of the way in the morning," thought Briar. *"Besides, everyone will be asleep by the time we get there should we continue tonight."*

The next morning, they checked out of their hotel & continued towards Danville. Everyone was ominously quiet perhaps because not only had Lily moved on, but this was their first assignment with Iris.

Upon reaching Danville, the Fatal Five split up to minimize suspicions among the locals. Each of them had multiple "targeted victims" but would choose a different location on the college campus to initiate the seduction of each target. Once the target was under the influence of either a succubus or incubus, the target would be lured to a secluded spot for multiple encounters until the target had all life force drained & the target died. The Fatal Five moved both inconspicuously & efficiently throughout the college campus until all their quotas were met. Just as quickly as they had descended upon the small college town, they retreated into hiding to rest & recover in the Pocono Mountains of Pennsylvania.

"Good job everyone," exclaimed Briar to Holly, Ivy, Iris, & Rose. "We are all free to relax and readjust to our enhanced life forces." Briar, Holly, Ivy, & Rose celebrated their successful campaign, but Iris retreated down to the jacuzzi to spend time in quiet contemplation. Ivy followed Iris down to the jacuzzi. Before getting too near, Ivy respected Iris & mildly feared her because of Iris' Marine & CIA training.

"Iris, may I join you?" asked Ivy.

"Why not Ivy? It's a free country," replied Iris. "Congratulations on a successful mission."

"Thank you, Iris! I did kick dick if I do say so myself!" exclaimed Ivy as she was quite proud of herself.

"What do you mean kick dick Ivy?" asked Iris.

"Oh, that's just a girl's response to a dickhead guy when he says cunt punt," explained Ivy.

"I see," said Iris.

"You were awesome as well Iris!" added Ivy.

"Thanks, Ivy," said Iris.

"But you don't seem too thrilled," offered Ivy.

"I'm not," answered Iris. "While these young boys are cute, they are just collateral damage."

"Then why are you doing this if you don't enjoy it & if you don't want to fully transform into a demon?" asked Ivy - curious now as to what made Iris tick.

"It's a means to an end. I don't really enjoy sex & I'm not interested in becoming a demon. Mangum & I reached an agreement that is mutually beneficial for both of our aspirations," explained Iris. "I agreed to help the Fatal Five temporarily & my targeted victims are actually credited to the rest of you guys. In return, I will be able to retain my human form with specific demonic powers limited to punishing some of the worst people that have ever lived."

"Iris, how do you know that you can trust him?" inquired Ivy.

"While in the CIA overseas, I interviewed various religious leaders. A Maulvi from a mosque in Riyadh, Saudi Arabia, a Rabbi from a synagogue in Tel Aviv, Israel, a Priest from the Vatican City, Rome, Italy, & a Minister from Cork, Ireland. I asked them all the same 20 questions. Specifically, when I asked them how to torture a demon, they all

agreed on the same method. That is why I can trust

Mangum because he knows I know how to torture

him; he knows better than to double-cross me. He is

a pain-in-the-ass demon, but he is not one of my

targets," replied Iris.

"I am so confused," said a bewildered Ivy.

"When I was serving my last tour of duty

in the Marines, I was assigned to a consulate in the

Gulf Region. The security was at best inadequate,

but repeated calls for more security were dismissed.

One night, insurgents stormed the compound, broke

into the consulate offices, & killed most of the

occupants. They knocked me unconscious because

there were too many of them for me to fight off. I

woke up blindfolded, bound, & gagged. I wondered

why they did not kill me, but when they were

through using me I wish that they had killed me," answered Iris.

"What do you mean used you?" asked Ivy.

"They tied me to the center post of a village hut out in the middle of nowhere. I was repeatedly gang-raped, sodomized, & forced to perform oral sex on the vilest, disgusting animals in that region. They held me captive for a year & half as one of their sex slaves," replied Iris – now visibly traumatized by the flashbacks & crying heavily.

"Oh my – that's horrible. No wonder you don't like sex! How did you survive such a horrendous ordeal?" asked Ivy.

"Somehow, someway, I knew that I had to stay alive long enough to exact my revenge," said Iris.

"But how did you escape?" inquired Ivy.

"One morning, I heard heavy gunfire outside & heard those ISIS bastards retreating as a battalion of resistance fighters in the area – they may have been Sunni Muslims – enter into the hut. They covered my body & untied me – then took me to a hospital & I was nursed back to health. They contacted the Department of Defense to arrange my return to the United States," continued Iris.

"My body healed much quicker than my mind or so I thought. After going through intense counseling to deal with the year & a half of hell, I thought that I was finally somewhat adjusted. After some injuries that would not heal, I was first diagnosed with rectal cancer & after going through treatment for it, I was then diagnosed with cervical cancer. I went through another two years of treatment & now, both cancers are in remission. After everything I had been through, the CIA approached me with an opportunity to go back overseas under much safer conditions to help fight sex traffickers – which they knew I would be in favor of.

"I agreed with specific stipulations. I needed the CIA assets to find out everything about the animals that had abused me - names, addresses, family ties, & associations. I also negotiated the CIA to sponsor my interview trips for Saudi Arabia, Israel, Italy, & Ireland.

"So now, once I have helped Mangum as agreed upon, he will bestow the aforementioned demonic powers. Then, it is PAYBACK TIME!" exclaimed Iris.

"You got that right!" agreed Ivy.

"Hell hath no fury like the scorn of a woman," said Iris.

The Fatal Five continued their seductive, lethal missions throughout the Northeast in Philadelphia, Newark, New York City, New Haven, Providence, & Boston. With the completion of the Boston mission, Iris had exceeded her quota. A few nights later, Mangum & Iris met alone at midnight on Nahant Beach less than an hour from Boston.

"Iris, you have performed admirably especially for a human & have exceeded our agreed-upon quota; therefore, I consider your obligations fulfilled. Now, I will bestow upon you the requested three demonic powers for you to use against your sworn enemies," declared Mangum. "You are free to go about your business." Iris gave Mangum a respectful nod & made her way back to Logan Airport, Boston & booked the next flight to Heathrow Airport, London.

Upon landing in London, she took a taxi to a CIA-owned apartment where she kept a small wardrobe of clothes & necessities. Once she got settled, she turned in for the night to get some rest before leaving London in a day or two. The next morning, Iris reached out to her CIA contacts & they sent her the requested intelligence on the names, addresses, family ties, & associations of the people who abused her years back. Through her prior work of breaking child sex rings in the region, she had forged working with relationships with several Muslim groups who opposed the brutal ISIS regime. Even al Qaeda decided to break ties with ISIS in 2014, rejecting the extremely radical group, & opposing their evil practices. Her Muslim contacts had provided Iris with the specific home addresses of Iris' eight targets in the following Iraqi towns of Amreli, Baqubah, Bazian, Hawija, Kalar,

Kirkuk, Makhmur, & Mandali. The first phase would be executed in the centrally located remote location of Beşiir Kasabasi.

Iris had acquired the three demonic powers from Mangum that would allow her to exact her most satisfying revenge. She now had Unnatural Strength power, Teleportation power, & Mind Control power.

Li Qiang, her old trusted friend from Singapore, would meet her at the hotel Dedeman Erbil where they were both staying in separate rooms. He had arranged shipment of his rattan canes to the hotel in discreet packaging. After both arriving at the Erbil International Airport, they both drove to Beşiir Kasabasi for Li Qiang to construct the A-shaped frame (called a "caning trestle") where each of the 8 abusers would be caned by Iris with her unnatural strength. Through her mind control, she manipulated the minds of all 8 men to come to an abandoned building in Beşiir Kasabasi & comply with all her commands. Iris had the minds of all 8 abusers in a fog. They willingly allowed Li Qiang to bind their wrists & ankles to the frame. Once they were all tightly bound to each caning trestle, she removed the fog from their minds to watch them panic in terror at the realization of their plight. They are started screaming & struggling to break free but to no avail. Li Qiang had seen many canings in his home country of Singapore & was an expert in both binding criminals to the caning trestles & administering caning as a form of corporal punishment.

"Okay Li, show me how it is done," said Iris. Li Qiang had let the rattan canes soak in water while constructing the trestles – these canes would inflict some significant pain. He pulled the cane back behind his right shoulder & swung with all his might hitting the first target squarely in the buttocks. The first target screamed & was writhing in pain. He repeated the same swing on the other seven men with the same reaction as they all screamed in pain. Every strike of the cane opened flesh wounds.

"Here you go Iris," replied Li Qiang. "It's payback time." Iris took a soaked cane in each hand & swung at each man with both hands with a force five times as hard as Li Qiang. All 8 men were screaming at the top of their lungs, crying, & trembling in pain. She shoved a 14" metal rod with sharp edges in and out of the rectum of each man as they shrieked in excruciating pain from the rod.

"HOW DO YOU BASTARDS LIKE BEING DRILLED IN THE ASS?" screamed Iris.

One by one, she had Li Qiang both untie & retie each man to the trestle, but this time facing Iris. She hit each man multiple times in the penis & scrotum with the canes causing them all to pass out from the pain.

"Li Qiang, I will move each of them to a holding cell in Erbil, then please burn down these trestles," said Iris.

"Iris, Erbil is almost two hours away. How will you manage to move these eight men?" asked Li Qiang.

"One of my new powers is Teleportation – which combined with Unnatural Strength allows me to move them quite easily," replied Iris. "Would you be my lookout while I take care of business?"

"No problem Iris," answered Li Qiang & turned his back toward the entrance of the abandoned building. Every 10 minutes, Li Qiang heard whoosh & felt a stiff breeze.

"Okay Li Qiang. Each of them is in their own holding cell," said Iris. "Phase One is done. Thanks for your help & I will see you soon." With that, Iris disappeared from Li Qiang's view & he torched the eight caning trestles, made his way back to Erbil, & the next morning took the first flight back home to Singapore.

Iris returned to the holding cells of the eight men. Through her Mind Control power, she delved into the psyche of each man to discover each man's greatest fear:

The first had Acrophobia, a fear of heights, so at midnight Iris teleported him to the top of the Burj Khalifa, Dubai, U.A.E. where he took one look down & died of intense fear.

Next, the second man had Pyrophobia, a fear of fire; Iris teleported him to Mount Etna, above Catania, Sicily & dropped him into the active lava below the volcano's rim burning him to death.

The third man had Lupophobia, fear of wolves; he was taken to Northern Siberia & forced to come face to face with a large pack of grey wolves that completely consumed him.

Next, the fourth man suffered from Galeophobia, an extreme fear of sharks; Iris forced him to go to Dyer Island, South Africa & she dropped him into a dense population of great white sharks & he was eaten alive.

The fifth man had Arkoudaphobia, the fear of bears; Iris teleported him to the Arctic Circle into a polar bear habitat where he was torn apart by an angry mother bear.

Next, the sixth man was plagued with Ophidiophobia, a fear of snakes; he was taken to semi-arid parts of central east Australia, the habitat for the most dangerous snake in the world, the inland taipan; with venom so toxic that it may be able to kill a minimum of 100 adult men. He was bitten by an 8-foot inland taipan & was dead soon thereafter.

The seventh man suffered from Claustrophobia, a fear of confined spaces: Iris forced him into a smuggler's long cave on the California/Mexican border & he asphyxiated due to a lack of oxygen.

Lastly, the eighth man had Hydrophobia, a fear of water; Iris teleported him to the Challenger Deep which is located under the western Pacific Ocean at the southern end of the Mariana Trench, southwest of Guam. Here, Iris's last target drowned in the world's deepest part of the ocean.

At long last, Iris regained a sense of self-worth & dignity. Some of her deepest wounds felt deeper than the deepest ocean & she would carry some scars for the rest of her life. Standing on a quiet beach in Guam, she hung her head & cried. She booked a flight to Arlington National Cemetery in Virginia to pay respects to her fallen comrades & honor the memory of those friends.

"This is a beautiful place," said an old male voice.

"Yes Sir, it is," replied Iris looking up to see an elderly man holding on to his walker with his elderly wife to his left. "I came to pay my respects to my band of brothers & sisters & to honor their memory."

"Likewise, for me young lady, although many of mine were laid to rest in Normandy after D-Day," stated an elderly man. Iris's eyes grew wide & she extended her hand. She had not met many World War II veterans!

"Sir, my name is Iris. It is truly an honor to meet you!" exclaimed Iris.

"We are Joe & Janice Smith. The pleasure is all ours," said Mrs. Smith. "Are you just visiting, or do you live around here?"

"I am on a mini-vacation but will be in town for a couple of weeks," answered Iris.

"Splendid," said Mrs. Smith. "We want you to come and stay with us! You & Joe can talk shop, or you can just spend time with me & my friends. We won't take no for an answer!"

"Very well," answered Iris. "*It will be nice to spend some time with some down-to-earth people for a change,*" thought Iris. "Thank you for your

hospitality." Iris smiled & her faith in humanity

slowly but surely began to be restored.

Chapter 3
Celestial Rage

"Wake up Jim! You overslept!" said Jen.

"Oh shit, that son of a bitch Wayne is going to be all over my ass again," said Jim.

"This will be the third time this month that I am late," thought Jim. *"I have to start sleeping better or I will lose my job."*

"It's okay Sweetie," said Jen. "Just let him know that the doctor had to change your meds & you are not sleeping well."

"Thanks, honey, but with the business slowing down, so they are just waiting for us to screw up," replied Jim. "They don't care about my two old projects from last year that helped turn the company around. I will start using the alarm on my cell phone since I can't rely on the old digital clock.

I got to jump in the shower & get ready to run out the door."

"May I make breakfast for you Sweetie?" asked Jen.

"No honey, I don't want you to be late for your doctor's appointment," answered Jim. "Just come on in the bathroom so we can both be getting ready at the same time." Jim quickly showered, threw on his clothes & grabbed his briefcase. Just as he was about to leave for work, Jen exited the bathroom wrapped in a towel.

"Jim, come kiss me goodbye first!" exclaimed Jen. Jim walked over & wrapped an arm around Jen then kissed her goodbye.

"Jen, call me when you get home from the doctor. I just want to know that everything is good with both you & the baby," said Jim. "Are you sure you don't want me to go with you to the doctor?"

"No Jim, we will be fine. You may want to go with us later for the ultrasound since it is our first baby together," replied Jen.

"I will plan on it then," said Jim. "See you tonight Honey."

"See you tonight Sweetie," replied Jen.

Jim's train arrived into the Grand Central Terminal on time & he was able to make the 10-minute walk to his office building in Manhattan, NYC; reaching his office shortly before 9:00am. He put away his overcoat & briefcase just as his executive assistant ducked into his office.

"Good morning Jim!" said Grace. She was considerably older than Jim & hoping to conclude her career working for him with her retirement just 2 years away.

"Good morning Grace. What's going on?" replied Jim.

"Wayne has scheduled a meeting regarding a new potential client & needs to pull together the team for input. He wants to submit the Request for Quote (RFQ) by the end of the week," explained Grace.

"He wants everyone in the main conference room at 10:00am," stated Grace.

"Thanks, Grace – I will be there."

"May I get you anything Jim?"

"Actually, yes Grace. Please get me a coffee, a bagel & a bottle of water."

"Will do Jim. By the way, how is Jen & the baby these days?"

"Jen has an appointment this morning with her OB/GYN for a routine exam – so hopefully all is well. Thanks for asking Grace. Jen thinks the world of you," replied Jim.

"I like her too Jim. She is a jewel! I will be right back with your coffee, a bagel, & a bottle of water."

"Thanks Grace."

Jen reached her doctor's office building just before 9:45am. As she approached the receptionist's desk, she was greeted by one of her doctor's staffers.

"Hello Jen!" exclaimed Beth.

"Hello Beth! How are you?" replied Jen - beaming at the thought of her baby.

"So, Jen... I need you to fill out a few forms. Have there been any changes to your health since your last visit?" asked Beth.

Jen pointed to her chest & replied "Well, these are swollen & a bit sore!"

Beth nodded & said "Once your breasts get

used to producing milk, the pain may subside. Do you plan to breast-feed your baby? That may help relieve some of the pressure..."

"I hope so Beth. I am certainly going to try."

"Wonderful, have a seat, Jen. Dr. Kelly's nurse will call you back soon," said Beth.

"Hi Jen, I am Kate - Dr. Kelly's nurse. I was out on medical leave during your prior visits," said Kate. "Come with me & we will check your vital signs. Then, Dr. Kelly will see you soon."

Kate checked Jen's vitals & recorded them on the forms.

Jen asked, "How is everything?"

"Well, your blood pressure is a little high as is both your cholesterol & triglycerides. If possible, you need to try to walk every day & eat a low-fat diet as much as possible," explained Kate.

"May I ask you a question, Kate? I read on the Mayo Clinic website that about 12 to 14 weeks of pregnancy that it may be possible to hear the baby's heartbeat. Is that true?" asked Jen.

"Actually, we do have a Doppler – which is a small device that bounces sound waves off of the baby's heart," answered Kate. "Would you like me to ask Dr. Kelly if we can try to listen for your baby's heartbeat today?"

"Oh, would you? I would love to hear it & I know Jim would love to hear it too!" proclaimed Jen.

"Okay, let me go ask him right now," replied Kate.

"Thanks Kate."

"No problem Jen."

After a few moments, Kate returned & smiled. "Dr. Kelly would be more than happy to listen for your baby's heartbeat once he concludes his primary exam."

"Hello Jen," said Dr. Kelly. "I have reviewed your vitals & agree with Kate that you need to try to walk every day & you will need to eat a more balanced diet. I will give you a detailed list of foods I want you to incorporate more into your diet as well as foods you need to avoid. Our concern is to avoid developing gestational diabetes. We want both you & the baby to come through the pregnancy with flying colors. We want to avoid any complications for both of you. Before we begin with the Doppler, do you have any questions for me?"

"Not at the moment Dr. Kelly," replied Jen.

"Very well. You have my business card if you have questions later, don't be afraid to ask. If I can't answer you immediately, I will reply to you as soon as possible," said Dr. Kelly.

"Kate, open up the application on the Doppler computer. Once you have it opened, we will start listening for the baby's heartbeat," stated Dr. Kelly.

"Jen, lean back on the exam chair & uncover your stomach. We are going to squirt a little gel on your belly to make the Doppler sensor glide," explained Kate.

The sound of the heartbeat beat through the Doppler.

"There it is!" exclaimed Dr. Kelly.

Tears of joy welled up in Jen's eyes & she forgot the discomfort in her breasts. She could not wait to tell Jim all about it.

Jen left Dr. Kelly's office & sat down on a plaza bench – elated at hearing her baby's heartbeat.

She called Jim's cell phone to share the news, but the call went to voicemail. She also tried texting him, but no reply. Jen left Jim messages & started on her way back home.

After Jim's meeting ended, he went back to his office & checked his messages. Jim immediately tried to return Jen's call but got her voicemail. He could not wait to see her in the evening after work to celebrate the good news, but his life was about to be turned upside down...

Javier had made his way up through Central America & because he was an illegal alien, he had to pay a coyote, a person who smuggles illegal aliens into the U.S., to sneak him across the Mexican – U.S. border. While avoiding the authorities, he hitched rides from the Texas border to New York City. He has started working residential construction in the city & was saving up to buy his own car. He had bought a bottle of tequila & was driving his cousin's car on the way to see his friend, but the bottle of tequila rolled off the seat & into the floorboard. Javier reached down to pick up the bottle, looking away for just a moment, & did not see Jen crossing the street in the pedestrian crossing. The car was going 50 mph when it struck Jen. A pedestrian on the sidewalk adjacent to the accident called 911 on her cell phone, but by the time both the ambulance & police had arrived, Jen & her baby were no more. Javier was taken into custody & taken to the local police station. He was to be booked & charged with Death by Motor Vehicle...

Jim exited the train station & was ecstatic to reach home. He stopped at the florist to pick up Jen's favorite flowers – purple lilies. Upon paying for the lilies, Jim cradled the bouquet in his left arm

& continued on his way home. As he approached his apartment, he noticed several police cars in front of his building. *"I hope no one is hurt,"* thought Jim as he entered the elevator. Once he reached his floor, he passed 3 officers in the hallway talking to his neighbors. As he made his way down the hallway to his home, several of his neighbors were visibly upset & his next-door neighbor, Mrs. Brown, was inconsolable. Jim was met by 3 more police officers at his door as well as Dr. Thomas (a Psychiatrist & Family Counselor). "Mr. Clark, we need to speak with you inside." said Officer DiCenza. As Jim unlocked his door & allowed both Dr. Thomas & the officers to enter his home first, he followed them inside his home & closed the door.

"Jen, honey, I am home," called Jim. "The police are here & want to talk to us. Jen, where are you? Let me go find her, I will be right back."

"Mr. Clark, I am Dr. Thomas," stated Dr. Thomas. "I am a Psychiatrist & a Family Counselor. I am afraid we..."

"Jen, Honey, please come out!" exclaimed Jim, who was now beginning to panic.

"Mr. Clark, we are here to help you. There was an accident. Jen was beginning to cross the street & a distracted driver hit her. Both she & the baby did not survive," said Dr. Thomas. "Mr. Clark, Jim, we are so sorry for your loss."

"Oh God no! No! No God No!" cried Jim. Suddenly Jim felt pain running down both arms & in his back. He then went into cardiac arrest & collapsed to the floor. Officer DiCenza immediately began to perform CPR. "Don't die on us Jim!"

exclaimed Officer DiCenza. Dr. Thomas called 911 & explained the situation to the 911 Operator while both Officer DiCenza & his partner Officer Santos took turns performing CPR.

Several hours later, Jim had been both taken & admitted to Mount Sinai Hospital. Because of both the trauma of the cardiac arrest & the heavy medications, Jim was in & out of consciousness over the next several days. He did not remember the frequent visitors: Dr. Kelly & his staff, his co-workers, Mrs. Brown, Dr. Thomas & Officers DiCenza & Santos all came by more than once to check upon him. Even his manager, Wayne, had stopped by to see Jim. His private room had several bouquets of flowers, get well cards & sympathy cards. The funeral for Jen would be postponed if possible in the hope that Jim could attend it. Jim eventually woke up & realized his hand was being held by Mrs. Brown, his elderly neighbor; she

wiped her eyes & yet struggled to compose herself.

Jen had been like a daughter to her & she loved

spending time with Jen.

Jim attempted to speak, but he could not

utter a single word. He could not understand why he

could not speak. A nurse came in to check his vitals

& record them on his chart held in the clipboard.

Moments later, Dr. Levin, the attending ER

cardiologist, stopped by to check on Jim. Dr. Levin

picked up Jim's updated chart & turned to Mrs.

Brown smiling & said "Thank you for visiting him.

He needs to know that he is not alone. His recovery

will have a higher probability of success if he has

people to show him that they care. I wonder if you

would mind stepping out & let me speak to Jim in

private."

"Certainly doctor, I will be out in the visitor lounge, but will return soon," replied Mrs. Brown.

"Thank you, Madam," said Dr. Levin.

"Jim, I am Dr. Levin the ER cardiologist, who along with the ER Team, cared for you when you first came in. Despite the cardiac arrest, there does not appear to be any permanent damage to your heart. However, we will more than likely need to order additional tests to make certain that your heart is not damaged. Then, we can map out the best course of action to ensure that you do not sustain another cardiac arrest. Before I make my other rounds, do you have any questions for me?" Jim tried to speak but was unable to talk. Dr. Levin placed a hand on Jim's shoulder & said "Don't worry Jim. We can get you a pen & pad to write on should you need it. I will be back to check on you later. And Jim, I am so sorry for your loss."

As Dr. Levin was about to exit Jim's hospital room, he was met by a distinguished woman at the door & he introduced himself. "Hello, I am Dr. Levin – Jim's cardiologist," said Dr. Levin.

"Hello, I am Dr. Thomas – Jim's family counselor & psychiatrist," replied Dr. Thomas.

"Dr. Thomas were you aware that Jim is unable to speak?" asked Dr. Levin.

"We were not aware since during our previous visits here Jim was asleep. Jim has experienced traumatic grief – which is a double shock to his mind. He has experienced a psychosomatic episode – a grief reaction manifested at the very least with the inability to speak. He may exhibit more types of grief reaction before he is well. His mind is trying to reconcile the unexpected losses of both his wife & his child. Now, we will not pressure him to talk, but will simply try to help his mind process the losses. Once we see progressions or breakthroughs with his mind, the improvements may unlock his ability to talk once again. I predict that he will need psychiatric help long after he has been discharged from this hospital. We may have to transfer him to a psychiatric facility until he can function on his own. Please consider conferring with me frequently as we navigate through his treatment," replied Dr. Thomas.

"My primary concern is to help Jim overcome these devastating losses," said Dr. Levin. "Therefore, I will be more than willing to frequently confer with you if it will help Jim. I am primarily here at Mount Sinai most days but do also assist at some of the other local hospitals. Should you miss me here, please feel free to either text me or email me & if I am unavailable to talk immediately, I will follow up with you as soon as possible. Here is my business card with all my contact information. There is a psychiatric department here & I understand that the Manhattan Psychiatric Center (MPC) is also nearby – should we need to go that route."

"Actually, my office is in the MPC, but perhaps we can utilize the psychiatric department here at the appropriate time," replied Dr. Thomas. "If Jim does not respond to treatment here after a reasonable amount of time, we can transfer him to the MPC for treatment continuance. Here is my card as well should you need to reach me in the interim."

As Dr. Thomas entered Jim's room, Jim turned to see who was in his room. "Jim, you may not remember me, but I am Dr. Thomas," said Dr. Thomas. Dr. Thomas shared with Jim her recommendation for his treatment but did not overwhelm him with expectations. Rather, they would endeavor to make improvements each day. She reiterated her sympathies to Jim & assured him that she would be there for him. After she recommended 3:00pm afternoon sessions, Jim nodded in agreement & Dr. Thomas left.

Just after midnight, Jim woke up as a nurse was making her rounds to check Jim's vital signs. She asked Jim if he needed anything. After he shook his head side to side, she smiled & said "Ring the call button on the control & I will come back as soon as possible. I will see you later, Jim."

"Jimbo! Wake up punk ass!" exclaimed Satan. Jim woke up & the devil was standing over his hospital bed. "Speech! Speech! Oh, that's right – you are trying to convince everyone that you can't talk. What's the matter – cat got your tongue?" Look Jimbo, I don't how to break this to you, but Jen was not pregnant with your baby – she was pregnant with Wayne's baby. They have been having an affair for months!" Jim became enraged & started to violently shake. Tears of anger were running down his face. "She was doing everything with Wayne – you name it, she was doing it: anal, bukkake choke, fisting & swallowing. Some sick, disgusting stuff even for me. That was a fine little slut that you married there Jimbo. I can't believe you would put a ring on a cheap thot like that Jimbo. What were you thinking? Thinking with your little head instead of your big head?

"I'll tell you what Jimbo, she has had more men run through her than a 100-year old stadium tunnel. If there was ever a bimbo that needed a tramp stamp tattooed on her lower back, it was Jen! In fact, Jimbo, you could have put the phrase 'Jimbo's bimbo' above the tramp stamp! She may have been your bimbo, but she was Wayne's bitch!"

Jim began going into a seizure & just as the nurse ran in to attend to Jim, Satan disappeared - elated that he had enraged Jim... Both the nurse & the doctor working the night shift quickly entered Jim's room & injected Jim with a sedative to not only bring the seizure under control but to help Jim sleep. Once Jim was sleeping peacefully, both the doctor & the nurse exited the room.

Just after dawn, Jim woke up & saw a tall, muscular being adorned in white clothing was looking out his window. The being turned around

& said, "Jim, don't be afraid for I am Raphael."
Jim looked at him puzzled & thought *"what are*

you?" Raphael spoke to Jim telekinetically *"Jim, I*

am an archangel & one of the most experienced

ones in dealing with Satan. I am here to set the

record straight. Jim, you must not believe anything

he said. They were all lies. He just wanted to

torment you. His celestial rage against humans will

remain until his demise is complete."

   "You mean that Jen was not running around

on me & that the baby really was mine?" thought
Jim.

   "No Jim, Jen was not running around on

you. You are the only man that she had ever been

intimate with... She loved you with all of her heart

& she loved her life with you," thought Raphael.

"She was so proud of you. She was proud of the fact

that you were a great provider to her & she truly

believed that you would have made an excellent father for your child."

Jim began to break down and cry; ashamed that he had doubted Jen & relieved that they had not been living a lie. Raphael put a hand on Jim's shoulder & said *"I am so sorry for your loss, but I also have an important message to give you. Regarding Jen & your child; they are watching over you & look forward to the day when you can all be together. That is not all. In cases where children die before they have grown up, they can grow up in heaven. That includes your child,"* explained Raphael.

Jim thought *"I want to be with them now."*

Raphael replied in thought *"Now is not your time Jim. God has other plans for you. It must be hard for you to understand right now, but you need to live the rest of your life here on Earth. Jen &*

your child will not have to wait long for you though,

but when you join them in Heaven, you will have the

rest of eternity with them. Would you like to know if

you either have a son or have a daughter?"

Jim reasoned *"Whether I have a son or a*

daughter, he or she is my child & I will love my

child just the same!"

"Good answer Jim! Good answer!" thought

Raphael.

Jim thought of more questions to ask

Raphael, but Raphael had already read Jim's mind.

"They are not suffering, they are not sad & they

know that you have unfinished business here on

Earth. Be strong Jim. Satan may come back

someday, but now you know the truth. Have faith,

remember your prayers, read the Scriptures & you

will neither falter nor fall."

"Thank you Raphael. Please tell my family that I love them," thought Jim.

Raphael turned to leave but looked back in Jim's direction. *"I will tell them Jim, but they already know. They love you too,"* replied Raphael. *"Until we meet again Jim."*

Chapter 4
One for The Road

Dan had been working at the same motorcycle repair in Kalispell, Montana for the last seven years. He could have already moved on, but he really liked his boss, Mr. Smith, because he paid Dan well, treated Dan right, and Mr. Smith knew motorcycles; so, the job was a good fit for Dan. Besides, Mr. Smith took a chance on Dan after Dan was honorably discharged from the Army after 2 deployments overseas; so, Dan felt a bit of loyalty to Mr. Smith. Dan was proud of his military service but was ready for a change and Mr. Smith obliged.

Kyle was a recent graduate from the Motorcycle Academy & even though he was young, he had won the approval of both Mr. Smith & Dan by working hard & being dependable. To them, Kyle was a good kid and with time, he would make an awesome gearhead. Kyle was humble and always asked a lot of questions. Even though Kyle had gone through the academy, he showed a ton of respect to both Mr. Smith & Dan by running a repair by them before tackling a job – just to make sure he was doing the repair jobs the right way and was not afraid to ask for help if he got stuck in a repair.

"Hey Dan, you got big plans for the weekend?" asked Kyle on a Friday afternoon in late August.

"Bro, I got a few more repairs on my motorcycle & hope to have it up and running by the end of the day tomorrow. Then, I want to take a ride south towards Missoula, Helena & maybe Butte on Sunday. Trying to get in some riding before the snow starts in a month or two. Once I put my bike away for the winter, I will be wishing I had ridden more while the weather was still good," replied Dan.

"Sounds like a solid plan Mr. Dan!" said Kyle.

"I am not so sure about Butte – probably depends on how I am feeling once I reach Helena," added Dan after thinking about the ride.

"Dan, if you get in a jam during the repairs – let me know. I got a few things going on in the morning, but I can break away in the afternoon if you need an extra set of hands," offered Kyle.

"Thanks for the offer Bro – I will keep that in mind," stated Dan.

"Alright, guys – time to call it a day. Thanks for your help & I hope you guys have a good weekend!" said Mr. Smith.

"Thanks, Mr. Smith – same to you," replied both Dan and Kyle as they went out the side door of the repair shop and got ready to drive to their respective homes.

The next afternoon, Kyle got a text from Dan "*Hey Bro, if the offer still stands, I could use your help for a few hours. Let me know. Thanx.*"

After a few minutes, Kyle replied "*NP, will be there in 20 minutes!*"

"*Good kid,*" thought Dan. "*He was raised right.*"

"Here goes nothing," said Dan as he kick-started his bike & throttle the gas a few cycles.

"Okay, I think we are in business. Thanks, kid! What do I owe you?" asked Dan.

"Not a thing Mr. Dan! I am grateful for you sharing your mechanic wisdom with me & I am glad to finally return the favor," replied Kyle.

"I guess you got a hot date tonight with a young lady," inquired Dan.

"No Sir. My parents are out of town this weekend & I got the house to myself – so it's a great time to work on rudiments, snap-ups, & experiment with drum-head modification. I am still trying to get back into playing mode and build up my endurance," replied Kyle. "I am also trying to listen to some of the old-school cats as well as looking for any music I can find with Gene Krupa, Buddy Rich, and those guys."

"Awesome. Once you put your band back together, I know a few club owners that are always looking for performing bands. I can put in a good word for you," explained Dan.

"Thanks, Mr. Dan!" exclaimed Kyle. "See you Monday!"

"You are welcome, Bro. Have fun drumming," replied Dan.

Dan walked out of his garage & pulled the garage door down. He walked into his house to eat an early dinner, pack his backpack for his Sunday bike ride, & to try to turn in early to ride out on his Harley first thing in the morning. The next moment, his cell phone rang & he saw that his Uncle Will was calling him from Reno, Nevada.

"Hello Uncle Will!" exclaimed Dan.

"Hey, Dan. How's it going? Did I catch you at a bad time?" asked Uncle Will.

"No Sir Uncle Will. Just getting ready to turn in early & take a bike ride down through part of Western Montana tomorrow. Is everything alright Uncle Will?" replied Dan.

"Yes, Dan – all is well. I have decided to retire & sell my motorcycle repair shop. I wanted to offer it to you first & I could work alongside you for a year or so to show you the ropes on the administrative stuff. I know you have the shop part down pat," said Uncle Will.

"Uncle Will. I am flattered & it sounds like an awesome opportunity," said Dan.

"But?" asked Uncle Will.

"But, I don't know if I could afford it," pondered Dan.

"Dan, I am having both my accountant & my attorney run the numbers to determine that fair market value of the business. They will probably determine the valuation in the next 30 to 45 days," stated Uncle Will. "I have built up a significant clientele & I am pretty sure that you can not only maintain it but also grow it a bit. Since I lost my boy Tommy in Afghanistan, you are my closest family member; so, it only makes sense for you to inherit a third of the business."

"Uncle Will! I don't know what to say?" exclaimed Dan.

"Just say thanks & that you will do it. Once we join up, we can set up a schedule where you buy the remaining two-thirds of the business over time," explained Uncle Will. "So, what do you think Dan? Are you interested?"

"Yes Sir I am!" replied Dan.

"Outstanding. Once my team calculates the fair market value, I will have them to draw up a proposed transfer of the business & all that will encompass the transition phases from the time you start until the transfer of the business is complete," continued Uncle Will. "We should be able to send you the paperwork within the next six to eight weeks."

"Thank you, Uncle Will! You are the best!" exclaimed Dan.

"Thank you, Dan. I am glad to know that the business will stay in the family. We will talk again soon," replied Uncle Will.

After dinner & packing his backpack, Dan went to bed to try to get some sleep before his ride the next day, but his mind was racing regarding his newfound fortune. His thoughts also kept going back to Saya, his beloved late wife, who he felt was always with him. He thought about her family too & what a horrific tragedy befell them at the hands of ISIS. Saya was his pride & enjoy; the woman he always dreamed of but never thought he would find. Through devastating destruction, they found each other 9 years ago & saw in each other a glimmer of hope & the chance for a better life together. It was her ability to speak English as well as the loss of her family that allowed Saya's citizenship application to be expedited through USCIS in Helena. They could have married in Iraq, but she wanted to get married in the U.S. with as many as Dan's family & friends as possible.

Dan's family & friends welcomed Saya with open arms & tried to help her any way they could. She had become a valued member of the Kalispell community & was considered a friend to most everyone that she met. Because she was so highly thought of in the community, her loss reverberated throughout Western Montana when she succumbed to cervical cancer two years ago. Before she died, she had expressed her desire to be laid to rest beside Dan – whenever that would be. While she was still alive, Dan bought two plots in Kalispell to give Saya peace of mind regarding her final resting place & even took her to see the serene place he had chosen with a beautiful view of the mountain scenery.

Eventually, he managed to drift off to sleep & slept through the remainder of the night until the alarm woke him up. After breakfast, Dan took his gear & loaded it in one of the side-saddles of his Harley. Once he had backed his bike out of the garage, he closed his garage door – locking both it and his house up before taking off toward Missoula. Dan drove down U.S Highway 93 towards Flathead Lake. Dan's day trip went according to plan & he hit all the stops that he had intended to make. He reached home about 8:00 pm MDT with still a couple of daylight hours left.

On Monday morning, he decided to tell Mr. Smith about his uncle's offer.

"Dan, as much as we are going to miss you around here, I am very happy for you & know you will seize this golden opportunity. I know you will be successful & I just want to thank you for your years of service with me. This is all of a sudden, but I will be flexible on your end date in the next two to three months," said Mr. Smith.

"Thank you Mr. Smith. I didn't plan on any of this..." replied Dan.

"Dan, no need to explain. These things happen sometimes. I do request that for the duration of your time with us that you & Kyle work closely together so he can absorb as much wisdom from you as possible," stated Mr. Smith.

"Will do Mr. Smith. Once I am gone, he can call me anytime if I can be of service," said Dan.

Six weeks had passed since Uncle Will had contacted Dan & Dan was concerned that the deal would not go through. However, when Dan reached home from work one weekday in October, he had an overnight envelope from an attorney's office in Reno, Nevada. Upon opening the envelope, Dan observed a formal letter from his uncle outlining what they had previously discussed. Both Uncle Will's attorney & accountant were on a courtesy copy. Both an airline voucher & hotel confirmation were also included for a round-trip flight from Kalispell to Reno & back – including a brief layover at the Sea-Tac (Seattle-Tacoma) Airport. The flight would depart on the upcoming Friday & return to Kalispell on Sunday evening.

A note from Uncle Will was clipped to the formal letter:

"Hi Dan, once you receive this please call me at your earliest convenience. I hope you don't mind that I set your travel arrangements; if we need to re-schedule for a different day/time, please let me

know & I will be more than happy to accommodate your preference. All the best! Uncle Will," was all the note stated.

Dan realized that the note was briefer & more direct than Uncle Will usually sounded. *"I hope that Uncle Will is well,"* thought Dan. Dan called Uncle Will at once.

"Hello Dan," answered Uncle Will. "Did you receive the overnight envelope?"

"Hi Uncle Will," replied Dan. "Yes, I did. The travel arrangements are fine – thanks for making the arrangements."

"It took a bit longer to draw up the paperwork as there have been some additional complications that have arisen. We will discuss it on Saturday morning. When you arrive in Reno Friday night, your hotel shuttle will be outside the D Doors North of the baggage claim. I will pick you up at the hotel at 10:00 am Saturday," said Uncle Will.

On Friday afternoon, Dan's connection flight from Kalispell reached the Sea-Tac Airport on time & without issues. On the plane to Reno, Dan found his aisle seat - stowing away both his carry-on & computer bag. He put in his earbuds & streamed music on his phone until time to take off & closed his eyes to get a few moments to relax. A short time later, Dan felt a gentle tap on his shoulder & woke to see a smiling young woman looking down at him.

"Hi! Sorry to wake you, I just need to get to my seat!" replied the gorgeous, shapely redhead continuing to smile at him.

"Oh, crap – my bad! I must have dozed off," said Dan as he got up from his seat to let the redhead take her seat. After she sat down, Dan

returned to his seat & was about to put his earbuds
back when the flight attendant asked for the
passengers to place their devices to airplane mode.
Dan just powered off his cell phone & stuffed the
earbuds in his coat pocket.

"Hi, I'm Ginger!" exclaimed the redhead
– extending her hand to Dan.

"Hi, I'm Dan."

"Nice to meet you Dan," continued
Ginger.

"Likewise," replied Dan.

"No offense Dan, but your hand is kind of
rough."

"Sorry about that Ginger – a side effect of
my line of work."

"So Dan, what is your line of work?"

"I'm a mechanic."

"What kind of mechanic?" asked Ginger.

"A motorcycle mechanic," replied Dan.

"That is so awesome Dan! A motorcycle mechanic," exclaimed Ginger. "Do you ride?"

"Oh hell yes – every chance I get. I am one for the road," replied Dan.

"Like down Interstate 5?" continued Ginger.

Dan shook his head. "No, I'm not from Seattle. I usually ride in Western Montana from my hometown of Kalispell down to Missoula & Helena... sometimes Butte... sometimes Bozeman."

"So you're a mountain man motorcycle mechanic," concluded Ginger.

"Hello. Would you care for something to drink?" asked the flight attendant.

"I will have a double gin & tonic," replied Ginger.

"I will have a ginger ale," replied Dan.

The flight attendant served them both & moved on down the aisle.

"No disrespect Dan but isn't that a wimpy drink for a mountain man?" suggested Ginger with a grin.

"Actually alcoholism is pervasive in my family – so I try to limit my intake to a minimum," said Dan.

"Besides, Saya would not approve," thought Dan. Dan withdrew & got very quiet.

"Dan, I stepped over the line – my apologies," said Ginger.

Dan nodded to her in silence & looked ahead towards the front of the plane.

As the flight attendant made her way past Dan & Ginger, Ginger ordered another double gin & tonic. After Ginger drank her second drink, she intently studied Dan & started to feel attracted to him. At that moment, the plane began to experience turbulence. Dan hated to fly & begin to get worried; his mother & father were killed in a plane crash years ago.

Ginger gently touched Dan's hand & said with a smile "No worries Dan. I can guarantee you that we will reach Reno safely."

"How can you be so sure Ginger?" asked Dan.

"Knowing the past, present & future is one of my talents," replied Ginger. "Under the main gift of Dreams."

"One of your gifts?" continued Dan.

"All witches have at least one of the six gifts: Air, Water, Fire, Earth, Mind, & Dreams. Some of us have more than one gift," replied Ginger.

Dan's eyes got big. "Wait, whoa, stop," exclaimed Dan. "You're saying you're a witch?!?"

Ginger patted Dan's hand "You catch on fast Danny Boy!"

"But how can that be?" asked Dan. "I thought witches were supposed to be ugly!"

"Dan, look at me!" exclaimed Ginger. "Do I look ugly to you? My skin is smooth, soft & supple, my eyes are sapphire blue, my breasts are perky & my measurements are 36, 24, 36. So I ask you again. Do I look ugly to you?"

"Far from it. You are quite beautiful," answered Dan.

"Some others say that I am the most beautiful witch in our coven," added Ginger.

"Witch coven!" exclaimed Dan.

"Damn straight," laughed Ginger. "Coven lovin'! Don't knock it until you try it!"

"My apologies for the stereotype. It was ignorant of me," said Dan.

"Dan, it is okay; I forgave you the moment you said it," replied Ginger. "Another gift I have is this gift of Mind. Which means I can read you like a book. I know your intentions, your emotions, & what kind of person you are. You're a good man Dan. I know you better than you know yourself. I know that after two years you are still grieving the loss of Saya. All I can tell you is that I am sorry for your loss & that Saya suffers no more. She is in a better place – trust me on this one."

"Thank you for the kind words & reassurances," answered Dan.

"You're welcome Dan. It is no coincidence that my airline seat is next to yours..." said Ginger.

"I don't quite understand Ginger."

"Well, you know in most of Nevada that prostitution is legal. Most of the hookers are just working girls trying to survive from one day to the next, but there is a minority of them that worship the devil. These are the ones that I came to warn you about. They think you are an easy target with your two years of grieving," continued Ginger.

"Wait. Don't witches worship the devil?" asked Dan.

"Is it possible that some witches worship the devil? Perhaps, but as far as both me & my coven, we most definitely DO NOT worship the devil," replied Ginger.

"Of course avoid the houses of prostitution, but also avoid the casinos, the nightclubs, & even the hotel bars. However, the most important thing is your heart healing from the loss of Saya. Believe it or not, I have both seen &

talked to her spirit. She is going to come to you in your dreams. Do not be frightened for she is coming to you out of love for you. She is going to tell you to move on with your life & she is going to encourage you to love again," stated Ginger.

"This is so unbelievable," said Dan as he felt his eyes tearing up.

"Dan, I have to warn you that evil forces may also try to communicate with you in your dreams if they see you talking to Saya. Do not believe their lies as they will try to break you down. Don't believe a word they say. Once you have moved to Reno for good, I will find you again. I have to go now," replied Ginger. Ginger bent down & kissed Dan on the cheek.

"Ginger, you can't drop all of this heavy shit on me & then leave!" exclaimed Dan.

"Dan, I have to go NOW to the restroom," replied Ginger. "Don't worry. I have a vested interest in you. If you get off the plane before I get out, I will see you soon."

Dan stood up to let Ginger out. Ginger smiled & caressed the side of his face with the back of her hand before turning to go the restroom.

Soon, the plane descended & landed without incident. After most of the passengers had exited the plane, Dan stood up & walked to the restroom where Ginger had entered. There was no one in the restroom & there was no exit in the back of the plane – Ginger would have had to walk past him in order to exit the plane, but she was nowhere to be found.

Dan thought to himself *"maybe Ginger is a witch or a magician,"* because she had disappeared into thin air. However, he somehow found himself trusting that he would, in fact, see her again. After Dan got his bags from the baggage claim, he found the D Doors & exited to the right where he was able to take the shuttle to his hotel. After checking in his hotel room, Dan showered & and went to bed – immediately falling into a deep sleep.

As Dan slept, he began to dream of Iraq at night. He felt uneasy as he sensed negative energy from a malevolent presence.

"Dan, why did you let Saya's family die? Aren't you this super-soldier that killed five ISIS members? Sure, you helped save your platoon, but you let her family cruelly die!" exclaimed the specter.

"Who the hell are you?" shouted Dan.

"Hell is right. Our home for now – us demons that is," said the specter. "I am Agramon.

Since you let her family die, you are going straight to hell & I will personally torment you!"

"Try it & see what happens – you punk ass bitch!" screamed Dan. "You don't know what happened to Saya's family. You're a fucking liar! Go back to hell!" At that moment, Agramon faded from view.

Dan then sensed dread & hopelessness – negative energy from another evil spirit.

"DANNY BOY! YOU'RE REAL PROUD OF YOURSELF – KILLING ALL OF THOSE INNOCENT IRAQI KIDS WITH YOUR RECKLESS ACTIONS & CARELESS DEADS. YOU WILL BE TORTURED IN HELL FOR YOUR TRANSGRESSIONS,"
yelled the demon.

"You are a mistaken demon," replied Dan. "That was not me. I never killed innocent kids."

"Really! Then why do you have such a strong sense of guilt if you have no blood on your hands?" continued the demon.

"I don't know who you are, but I never said I had no blood on my hands. I said I never killed innocent kids!" exclaimed Dan.

"I am Amducious the destroyer & I will destroy you," replied the demon.

"More like Amducious the dickhead. Go fuck yourself!" said Dan. Amducious then ran away.

Dan was shaking but was able to calm down even while in a deep sleep. Then, as he was entering the Iraqi city, Erbil, the capital city of the

Kurdistan Region, he sensed an alluring &
seductive sensation.

"Dan! Dan! Dan! Do we have the girls
for you!!!" exclaimed a mysterious male voice.
"Some of the finest women in all of the Middle
East," added a strange female voice. "We are here
to ensure that you have a night of unbridled
pleasure!"

Dan could only make out in the shadows
the silhouettes of both masculine & a feminine
figure.

"I am Ashtaroth, the goddess of lust &
seduction," said the female voice.

"And I am Naamah – which means
pleasing," replied the male voice.

"No offense, but not interested,"
answered Dan.

"C'mon Dan. Saya has been dead & buried for two years now – she won't care if you enjoy some of the local ladies of the evening. You must be about to burst at this point – two years of pent-up frustration!" exclaimed Ashtaroth.

Dan took a step forward towards them & stammered "Well I...", but then stopped himself. "No, no, no… I won't betray the memory of Saya."

"What are you gay Dan?" exclaimed Naamah.

"C'mon Dan. Don't be a pussy – that is what these ladies are for!" cried Ashtaroth.

"Not me. Not tonight. Not ever!" answered Dan. "Both of you need to get lost. I won't succumb to your devious ruses." Both demons departed from Dan.

At once, the night gave way to a day in Dan's dreams, but now he was no longer in Iraq; instead, he was back in Kalispell – not far from Saya's final resting place. All of a sudden, now Dan felt warmth, love, & peace. Saya appeared to him, not in her sickly state, but beautiful, healthy, & glowing.

"Hello my darling Dan," said Saya with a smile.

"Saya?!?" asked Dan – overwhelmed with mixed emotions. "*How can this be?*" pondered Dan.

"Oh Dan, I did not come to make you sad, but I have come to for other reasons. I have seen my family & they send you their blessings. They appreciate everything that you did for me while I was alive & they love you as a son – no matter what, you always be a part of our family."

With tears streaming down his face, Dan exclaimed "I miss you so much. Each day is a struggle to live, to take another step, & to breathe another breath. Everywhere I go, I see your face. I feel your tender touch with the wind on my face. Sometimes the pain of losing you is too much to bear."

"My love, that is why I wanted to tell you I have watched you struggle to move on. You have honored me by remembering me & being faithful to me even in death. I will always love you & I know you always love me – that will never change. We will always be connected," continued Saya. "However, I want you to move on now – you have grieved for two years & if you continue to grieve, it will be to the detriment of your health. I want you to live a long, healthy, & happy life. Someday, when your life here is over, we will be together once more."

"But how am I supposed to do that?" asked Dan.

"With Ginger," answered Saya.

"Ginger is a witch, so I don't know about that," replied Dad.

"Yes, she is, but she is so much more. She & I have talked at length. She possesses three of the six gifts of a witch: Dreams, Mind, & Water. In summary, she is loving, calm, intelligent, caring, observant, logical, sympathetic, & a problem-solver. She has the qualities that will help you & she understands you almost as well as I do. She says that there are not many good guys left anymore & that once she observed you, she knew that you were the man for her. Out of respect for me, she asked my permission to be with you in matrimony & after getting to know her, I gave her my blessing. Now, I give you my blessing – should you decide to marry again, she is the one that you need to marry.

"When you wake up in the morning, your perception will be changed & you will enjoy life again. I will be watching over you & will be waiting for you. I love you. Goodbye, for now, my love," said Saya.

"I love you too Saya. Goodbye for now," replied Dan.

Dan woke to the sound of the front desk wakeup call & after breakfast, he got ready to meet his Uncle Will downstairs.

A few moments before 10:00 am, Dan saw his Uncle Will about to enter the hotel's main entrance & he walked over to meet his uncle.

"Hello Uncle Will!" exclaimed Dan.

"Hey Dan," replied Uncle Will. "I trust you had a safe journey down here & that you slept well last night."

"I did have a safe trip & even though I slept some, I did have some disturbing dreams," said Dan.

Uncle Will nodded & said, "Yes, we were afraid of that."

"We?" asked Dan.

"Yes, Ginger & I," answered Uncle Will.

"You know Ginger?" asked Dan.

"Yes, I am responsible for booking her seat next to yours," replied Uncle Will.

"Uncle Will, how do you know her?" asked Dan.

"Dan, I have known her all of her life. I served with her father, Sam, in Vietnam," answered Uncle Will. "Sam made it back from the war, but he died of cancer a number of years ago – from chemical poisoning. In many ways, he had a much crueler death than some of the guys that did not make it back from Vietnam. The whole ordeal was catastrophic to his family. His wife died of a heart attack a few years later. Ginger went through hell from losing both parents & she kind on bounced around to a couple of foster homes. When your Aunt Marie & I got wind of her predicament, we offered to become her legal guardians & she accepted. It helped that she knew us from all of the socializing we used to do with her family – so there was a comfort level that Ginger had with us.

"We tried to provide her with a loving, supportive environment; structured, but we tried not to smother her & we tried to give her some freedom. She never got into major trouble; but we did have some challenging times the first year or so

– until she realized that we were not going anywhere & would not abandon her. In time, she began to trust us more & more all the way to adulthood.

"When she finished college, she married her high school sweetheart. He was an Army Ranger but was killed in Afghanistan less than a year after they were married & he was laid to rest at Arlington National Cemetery in Virginia. Her faith was shaken to the core & she kind of stumbled across a couple of witches that belonged to a local coven. She began to drink heavily but is coming out of a lot of that now. Ginger has a good heart – she just lost her way there for a while. She is coming around now & is ready to live her life again.

"Over the years, she heard me talk about you & she took a shine to you from afar. She has turned away countless suitors because she only has eyes for you, Dan. Don't feel pressure to reciprocate, but despite everything, she is an outstanding young woman. Trust your dear ole' uncle, there are not many around like her. Just think about it & if you are interested in her, you might want to make your move sooner rather than later."

After they reached Uncle Will's motorcycle repair shop, Uncle Will showed him around both the shop & the office area. Uncle Will gave Dan an overview of his business administration & Dan looked overwhelmed.

"Don't worry Dan – it seems overwhelming now, but in time, you'll get it all down pat. We need to go meet with my attorney & my accountant – both have been with me for years & have always done right by me. Afterward, we have reservations at a great restaurant & you'll get a chance to meet both the shop crew & the office staff; I've asked them to give you a chance. When I first told them about my retirement plans, they were all quite concerned. However, once I told them how much experience you have & your military service, they all felt a little more comfortable with the whole idea," explained Uncle Will.

The next 24 hours passed in an instant. Late Sunday afternoon Uncle Will had just dropped Dan off at the Reno Airport. Dan now wished that he had gotten Ginger's phone # from Uncle Will – so he could at least call her to "break the ice."

After making his way through Security, he found a seat near his gate both to charge his phone & check his messages before boarding his plane back home.

Shortly after settling into his seat near his gate, Dan got a text message *"Hi Dan, it's Ginger! I meant to give you my cell# - since I have your #!*

LOL! :)"

"*Hi Ginger! I meant to ask you for it...*

haha," replied Dan.

"*No problem – I'll see you on the plane.*"

texted Ginger.

"*What?!? You're going to be on this*

flight?" asked Dan.

"*Yes, I'm going back home. I live outside*

of Seattle in a cabin near the woods. I like my

privacy! :)" answered Ginger.

"*Awesome! I'll see you on the plane*

Ginger," texted Dan.

Dan made his way onto the plane, found

his assigned seat next to a window & got settled in

for the flight back through Seattle.

Moments later, Ginger approached her
aisle seat & saw Dan looking out his window.

"Hello Dan!" exclaimed Ginger.

"Hello Ginger!" replied Dan – standing up
to give her a hug. "Ginger, you were right about
everything, but I had no idea that you were a
widow. I am so sorry for your loss as well. It seems
that we have more in common than I first thought."

"Thank you. I have seen more than my
share of heartache too between the loss of both
parents & the loss of my husband but thank God for
your Uncle Will & Aunt Marie. I don't know where
I would be now without them taking such good care
of me for all of these years. They are so caring &
loving that they literally saved me from a terrible
future. I consider them my parents and they treat me
like their own daughter. I visited with Mom this
weekend while Dad was going over the business

with you. I didn't want to interfere since Dad needed the time with you."

"Ginger, I know that I want a future with you and although we just met, I do feel a special bond with you. Both Saya and Uncle Will told me all that I needed to know about you," said Dan. "The time and the place may not be ideal, but all I know is that I want to be with you now."

Dan reached into his coat pocket and pulled out a ring box. As he opened it and turned back to Ginger and asked "Ginger, will you marry me?"

As tears welled up in Ginger's eyes, she exclaimed "Yes! Yes! Yes!" After Dan placed the engagement ring on Ginger's left ring finger, they kissed & hugged for several moments.

"I was afraid that I had been too aggressive & chased you off," continued Ginger. "I have wanted this to happen so much but was beginning to doubt that we would ever be together. But Dan, how were you able to acquire a ring so quickly?"

"Uncle Will wanted to keep his mother's ring in the family. He wanted to give it to me to give to you, but I insisted that I pay for it in light of all that he has already done for me. Now you know that we will soon be together. We will inform Uncle Will & Aunt Marie as soon as we land, but before I board the flight back to Kalispell. We can set a date once we are able to coordinate our schedules, but I hope we can marry as soon as possible. I don't want to be without you any longer than we have to be, but we will make it work I promise!" replied Dan.

"I trust you Dan & I know you will do your best to pull it all together," said Ginger.

Over the next several months, Dan did pull it all together. He sold his place in Kalispell for a song to Kyle as a way to pay forward the good fortune that had come Dan's way. Ginger decided to keep her cabin outside Seattle as a vacation getaway for her & Dan. Dan & Ginger got married in a small chapel at Lake Tahoe & spent their 2-week honeymoon near Lake Tahoe; then they found a modest home just outside of Reno. Uncle Will was amazed at how quickly Dan picked up on the administrative side of the business & Uncle Will was able to retire in less than a year. Ginger sold her accounting firm in Seattle & opened an accounting firm in Reno with a number of great referrals gained from her former clients in Seattle.

In the end, both Dan & Ginger got the love & companionship they had both been missing. Uncle Will & Aunt Marie were not only able to enjoy retirement life, but also spent a lot of time with Dan & Ginger as a true family.

Chapter 5
Chasing the Dragon

"We are so sorry for your loss," was repeatedly conveyed from a procession of the wake attendees expressing sympathy to the parents of Keri Kemp – a beautiful high school junior who died of an accidental drug overdose, but also displayed symptoms of an allergic reaction. Keri had been the Kemps' pride & joy for all of her life. Not only had she been an outstanding student-athlete, but Keri also had been very popular in her school because she had a caring, good heart. She always tried to help the school kids less fortunate than herself.

The next afternoon, Ben & Lois Kemp attended the funeral of their only child – lost in disbelief, shock, & shattered hearts, but they tried their best to hold themselves together at least until they could reach home. Ben & Lois temporarily felt

a bit of comfort from the number of high school

kids that expressed their love & admiration for Keri.

The high school seniors respected Keri for the way

she carried herself – many stating that Keri was

"wise beyond her years." Both the sophomores &

the freshmen looked up to Keri & valued her input

in helping them with their problems – appreciating

how she always would take a few minutes to listen

to them. Her fellow juniors considered her to be the

best of all of them & they were the most distraught,

brokenhearted kids that they had attended either

Keri's wake or her funeral. Some distance away in

the memorial park, Ben noticed a shy & loner type

of girl leaning against a tree watching the funeral &

had intended to speak the girl afterward.

Ben had recalled that Keri had told him

about a shy, loner type of girl named Susan. Keri

had told her mom & dad that Susan was anti-social in large crowds because of bullying at an earlier age, but that if Keri talked to Susan one-on-one, Susan would open up & talk to Keri. Ben suspected that this girl was in fact Susan. As the funeral procession had mostly departed, Ben turned to go speak to the shy girl, but she was gone.

Ben & Lois held each other & slowly turned from their daughter's gravesite to make their way back to their car. On the way home, both were silent as they tried to not only process what just happened but grappled with what they could have done to save Keri. Their hometown of Huntsville, Alabama had been the idyllic setting in which to lay down their roots given that it was a melting pot of people from not only all of the U.S. but people from all over the world. Huntsville in many ways had offered the Kemp family exposure to multiple cultures which they felt would make them more well-rounded & would serve them well when traveling to other parts of the world. Huntsville was also home to the University of Alabama-Huntsville, Redstone Arsenal, & Mitre, as well as many companies supporting both the Department of Defense & NASA. The parents of Keri's friends were engineers, researchers, scientists, & other professionals who demanded that the area schools provide a rigorous curriculum for their children. Keri had loved her schools; even though they were rigorous, she had friends from many different places & different walks of life.

In rearing Keri, Ben & Lois tried to strike a balance between guiding Keri & also encouraging her to take responsibility for her commitments in both academics & athletics. Keri had become quite skilled in both time management & setting priorities, but should she ever feel overwhelmed, Ben & Lois had always guided Keri through the most stressful times.

After Keri's devastating injury on the basketball court eight months ago, her parents sensed Keri slowly drifting away from them & they suspected that the prescribed painkiller Oxycodone was the beginning of the end for Keri. While they did not want Keri to be in pain while she healed, they were also concerned with the risk of her becoming addicted. As the pain from her injury eventually diminished, her addiction to the Oxycodone remained. After increasing the dosage with each subsequent refill from 10mg, 20mg, & 40 mg, her physician gave her only 1 refill for OxyContin 80mg. She was trying to re-create the euphoric sensation of the first dosage of OxyContin, but it eluded her even as each subsequent prescription became stronger. Keri was now "chasing the dragon."

It was the refill of OxyContin 80mg which took over Keri's life. She was extremely drowsy through most of her classes. Keri felt too weak to participate either in any sports or any extracurricular activities. Her pupils were pinpointed. Keri's breathing was shallow. She had fainted several times & once on the stairwell at school but was caught by a football player before hitting the steps. As her prescription for OxyContin 80mg ran out, one of her former basketball teammates, Vanessa, gave Keri the contact information of a drug pusher in downtown Huntsville who sold "generic OxyContin 80."

Keri texted the drug pusher & told him what she was looking for.

After an hour, the drug pusher texted her

back "*$500 for a week's supply or $1,800 for a*

month's supply. We don't need your name or photo,

but give us your age, race, gender & any known

allergies."

Keri texted back "*17, Caucasian, female &*

pesto, pine nut, & shellfish. I will need a week's

supply to start," without questioning the motives or

intentions of the drug dealer; she just wanted more

OxyContin.

"*Send the $500 to PayPal Account*

PANAMAJACK1," replied the drug pusher. "*Once*

the money is in my account, I will send the medicine

to a PO Box here in Huntsville & will instruct the

post office to issue you the PO Box key."

"*Another white bitch,*" thought Luis

Cortes. "*Baal will be happy with this sacrifice & I*

will take out as many of these white bastards as

possible." Cortes had seen many of his family &

friends either jailed, deported, or killed trying to

illegally enter the U.S.; so far, he had avoided

deportation, but he knew it was just a matter of time

before he would get caught. Besides, he was trying

to impress the gang leaders & get initiated into the

gang brotherhood.

"*Fuck American laws,*" thought Cortes.

He was enraged that his people could not come &

go as they pleased. "*We have been entering

America for centuries!*"

"We have a white bitch to kill," said

Cortes to his lab crew. "Mix half OxyContin 80,

one-eighth crack cocaine, one-eighth pesto, one-

eighth pine nut, & one-eighth dried crab. Same look

on the pills as the real OxyContin 80 tablets. The

bastards won't know if the drugs killed her or the

allergens killed her, but either way, she'll be dead by this time next week."

Keri transferred the money from her savings account to the PANAMAJACK1 PayPal account. Two hours later received a reply from PayPal that PANAMAJACK1 had confirmed payment & had filled her order. PayPal also informed her that her order would ship to the Downtown Huntsville Post Office, PO Box 10666. USPS also texted her with a QRC barcode once the parcel was transferred to their location. Keri had been instructed to present it to a postal clerk at the customer service counter, pay a key deposit & she would be loaned a PO Box key for 1 hour. Upon receiving the QRC barcode on her smartphone, Keri drove to the Downtown Huntsville Post Office & stumbled into the post office. She tried to move as normal as possible, but she was excited to get more

OxyContin 80. Keri impatiently stood in line &

once she went to the customer service counter, she

paid the key deposit.

"When you finish, just walk right up to the

first window on the left & drop the key. We will

credit the deposit amount back to your debit card,"

stated the postal worker. Keri took the key &

located PO Box 10666, unlocked the box, &

removed her parcel. "*No return address,*" thought

Keri. "*These guys are not stupid.*"

Keri immediately returned the key & made

her way out to her car – a black Honda Civic gave

to her by her parents. "*I just want to get in the car &*

take a hit now," thought Keri. After entering her car

& closing the door, locking it, she ripped open the

padded envelope to find a normal-looking

prescription bottle. Upon opening the bottle, she

saw that these pills looked EXACTLY like the

prescribed pills from her doctor. Keri opened her bottle of water, took one of the pills & washed it down with a big drink of water.

Initially, Keri felt the same familiar euphoric relaxing sensations, but then she felt extreme pain in her chest, back, & down both arms. She also felt whelps on her arms, legs, face, & neck. Her tongue felt weird & her chest constricted. Keri's blood pressure bottomed out & she lost consciousness. A Huntsville police officer on patrol saw Keri unconscious & that she had symptoms of an allergic reaction. He used his nightstick to break the window & tapped her shoulder to wake her up but couldn't wake her. He immediately contacted dispatch & explained the situation. Within moments, an ambulance appeared on the scene & transported Keri to the Huntsville Hospital for Women & Children. Hospital staff immediately notified Keri's parents who rushed to the hospital. Shortly after arriving at the hospital, the ER doctor went to the waiting room to regretfully inform them that Keri had passed away – explaining everything that he had observed.

Given the unusual combination of symptoms, the doctor requested permission to perform an autopsy on Keri, but in his acute despair Ben turned down his request.

"What's the use," cried Ben. "Our baby is dead."

"We are so sorry for your loss, but we are just trying to determine the cause of..." replied the ER doctor.

"Ben, we owe it to Keri to get to the bottom of this..." said Lois.

"Do it, but only share your findings with both us & law enforcement," asserted Ben. "Here are our business cards for both me & Lois. Please

let us know the moment you have more

information."

"We certainly will," assured the ER

doctor.

Ben & Lois suffered through both the

wake & the funeral without Keri's autopsy results.

Their anger, grief, & broken spirits tested the

conviction of their marriage, but they remained

committed to one another & lifted up one another.

They tried to eat dinner one night but found that

they didn't have much of an appetite. However,

they knew that in order to be strong they had to take

care of themselves & both ate half of what they

would normally eat. After dinner, they opened a

bottle of wine & moved to the living room couch

with the only lights from both a small lamp in the

right corner & from the firewood burning in the

fireplace. Ben & Lois held hands & slowly sipped from their wine glasses staring at the flames of the fireplace in quiet retrospect of Keri's memory.

After the wine was consumed, both Ben & Lois smelled a strange burning smell different than the smell of the burning firewood. A dark sinister shadow with a reddish outline on the silhouette appeared to both of them to the left of the fireplace. They both let out a gasp & Lois squeezed Ben's hand & then hugged him as tight as she could – while tightly closing her eyes & burying her face in Ben's chest.

Ben stared at the malevolent shadow as it hissed, growled, & laughed a sadistic laugh.

"We are really enjoying your Keri in hell! She can fuck & suck with the best of them," exclaimed the demon. "How long has she been whoring herself out?"

"YOU'RE A DAMN LIAR, YOU DAMN SHIT FOR BRAINS!" screamed Ben at the top of his lungs.

"It looks like Lois taught Keri how to be a whore!" answered the demon.

"GO STRAIGHT BACK TO HELL YOU LYING FUCKING BASTARD & MAY GOD RIP YOU FROM LIMB TO LIMB," screamed Lois as loud as she could.

"You will soon learn that Keri had many drugs in her when she died. How do you think she paid for them? By giving blowjobs & anal sex, that's how! She was such a slut!" declared the demon.

"GO BACK TO HELL YOU ARE LYING BASTARD," screamed Ben. "YOU WEAK ASS DEMON!"

"Weak ass demon? Mortal scum! I am Baal – one of Satan's oldest demons!" replied the demon Baal.

"Baal? Isn't that Hebrew for sissy ass inferior demon?" Ben asked Lois in an attempt to distract Baal.

"Now you die mortal scum!" exclaimed Baal as he charged toward Ben – not seeing the vile of Holy Water that Lois had quietly grabbed from the end table.

Just as Baal was about to overtake Ben, Lois sprayed Baal with the Holy Water. Baal let out a high-pitched screech & disappeared into the darkness.

Ben & Lois embraced each other tightly – not believing what they had just witnessed.

"Oh God! Oh God! Oh God! Oh God!..." repeated Lois trembling uncontrollably.

"What are we going to do?" asked Ben.

In an instant, they both sensed a quiet calm & peace that enveloped them both. A soft glowing light replaced the dark sinister shadow & now they saw a white figure whose face became visible. Ben & Lois fell to their knees on the floor with their eyes closed & faces to the floor as both trembled uncontrollably. Ben & Lois both felt a gentle touch on their shoulders.

"My fellow servants of God. Do not fear me for I am the Archangel Gabriel & I have come to tell you truths. Do not believe Baal for he always lies," stated Gabriel.

"It is true that Keri was addicted to OxyContin, but it was not an illegal drug; unfortunately, she simply developed a dependency she could not overcome without intervention. She was a good girl in almost every way & she was a virgin when she passed away; she was determined to save herself for her future husband," added Gabriel.

"Then why didn't she tell us about the addiction? We would have gotten her the help she needed!" cried Lois.

"Keri was ashamed of her addiction & didn't want to disappoint you," answered Gabriel.

"We never believed that she had lost her virginity. We had given her a promise ring to help her remain chaste even in the most tempting of times," explained Ben. "We were trying to give her the best chance of a long, happy marriage someday."

"Keri wants you to know that her friend Susan will reluctantly contact you even though she suffers from social anxiety. Once Susan is able to overcome her anxiety, she has some important information to share with you," said Gabriel.

"Was Susan in any way responsible for Keri's death?" asked Lois.

"Not at all," answered Gabriel. "Susan is very observant & remembers events in great detail, but she is fearful for her safety at all times due to the bullying she suffered at an earlier age. Please be patient with her, not only for the vital information that she has retained in her mind, but she is also in dire need of help. You both must know that she was a good friend of Keri & they loved each other as sisters."

"We will help Susan any way we can," replied Ben.

"While Keri wants those responsible to be brought to justice, she wants you to know that she is in a happy place & is with your ancestors who have passed on before you. She loves you both very much & knows that you will all be together again someday," stated Gabriel.

"Thank you Gabriel!" exclaimed Ben.

"God bless you Gabriel!" exclaimed Lois.

"God bless you both as well," replied Gabriel. "Stay strong, support & love each other, keep the faith, & don't lose hope."

Luis Cortes pulled his pants back up after having sex with an illegal immigrant hooker. Cortes did not use a condom & he was reckless for not protecting himself or others – he just wanted to get laid. The Central American hookers were more submissive than the American hookers & because they were illegal, he could choke, punch, & slap them without retaliation or so he thought. Cortes drove his friend's car to a downtown back alley &

let Ana, the Central American hooker, out of the car.

"These bitches won't say a word or will call ICE on them myself," thought Cortes & laughed an evil laugh. Little did he know that the hooker made a deal to help ICE catch Cortes; in exchange, ICE would help her remain in the U.S. & become a U.S citizen. They also would help her escape her destitute life of prostitution & poverty. Ana had been with Cortes before & knew that he never made her take off all of her clothes; he just made her lift her dress. One of the opaque buttons on her dress was a camera lens & two other buttons were microphones to capture his image & his voice; ICE just needed his address. The car that Cortes was driving did not belong to him, but they could use the car license plate to track him from various traffic cameras. Now that Ana helped capture his

ugly face, ICE drones will be able to follow him to his address; he just didn't know it.

After Cortes pulled away, ICE officers surrounded Ana & took her to safety. Then, ICE drones followed the car to the outskirts of Huntsville where Cortes parked the car behind a storage building. ICE officials contacted FBI officials & shared all of the Luis Cortes data – including his current address. A task force from both agencies approached a Federal judge to obtain a search warrant for Luis Cortes's address. After reviewing the case file & finding substantial damning evidence, the Federal judge issued the search warrant. ICE drones confirmed that Cortes was still home at the current address. The FBI/ICE Task Force converged on the home of Cortes.

Agents knocked on the front door & shouted "FBI, OPEN UP!" As they heard the sound of guns being cocked, agents took safe positions to the left & right of the front door right before bullets riddled the door. Agents from all four sides of the house shot tear gas into every window & secured every conceivable escape. Moments later, the front door opened & three Panamanian men walked out screaming "Don't shoot! Don't shoot!"

ICE Officers Fernandez, Mendoza, & Perez took down the three Panamanian men in a most violent fashion. All three officers migrated to the U.S. years before & followed the immigration law to become U.S. citizens & loved their new country. These three animals made it harder for good, hard-working, law-abiding Hispanics to be accepted in their new country.

"Motherfuckers! Why did you slam us to the floor? You violated our civil rights!" screamed Cortes.

"You're not a U.S. citizen & you don't have any civil rights," yelled Fernandez. "You don't have any right to be here," Fernandez punched Cortes in the stomach as hard as he could. Fernandez HATED illegals – ESPECIALLY the criminals.

All three illegals were loaded into an ICE van & taken to a holding area within the FBI facility in Huntsville. As they were being processed, the three Panamanians were disruptive & uncooperative. Agents began to use tasers to make the prisoners comply. Each prisoner was placed in solitary confinement until they could be sentenced to state prison. Authorities did not want the prisoners transferred to a sanctuary state & set free.

"We serve Baal & Satan! You will burn in hell for how you have treated us!" screamed Cortes as all agents ignored his threats.

The ER doctor received the coroner's autopsy for Keri Kemp & forwarded it to both the Kemps, the Huntsville Police, & the FBI. While ICE had been dealing with the three Panamanian illegals, the FBI agents cataloged & photographed every room in the home. In addition to finding the narcotics lab, they found OxyContin, marijuana, cocaine, heroin, LSD, & poppy plants. They also found a collection of known allergens, a venom collection from scorpions, snakes, spiders, & poisonous frogs, as well as poisonous chemicals. The FBI concluded that this was a true house of horrors & was the creation of some truly evil people.

Special Agent Khan was chosen to write up the report from all of the agents at the site of the home. After completing his report, it was submitted to the Huntsville Bureau Chief & then it was

submitted to Quantico, VA to be added to the FBI's

National Database. A few days later,

Keri Kemp's autopsy report was forwarded to

Special Agent Khan with a post-it note outside the

manila envelope with the question "Does this

square with the raid of the Cortes home?" Special

Agent Khan opened the envelope to review the

autopsy with a pang of sadness. *"My God, she was a*

friend of my daughter Sonia. It could have been

Sonia instead of Keri," thought Khan. As he

reviews the autopsy, he also brought up the report

on the Cortes home. In a startling revelation, he was

convinced that Keri didn't die by accident – she was

murdered by a sadistic, evil group of people.

Special Agent Khan went to discuss it with the

Assistant Director Williams who concurred with

Khan. One of the three illegals was the mastermind

& would be charged with the first-degree murder of Keri Kemp. The other two illegals would be charged as accessories to murder. All three would be charged with possession of each narcotic found on the premises as well as illegal possession of guns. The challenge would be to get the two accomplices to rat on the mastermind.

The Bureau in Huntsville had an MMA instructor named Vinny that was an excellent interrogator who had a penchant for being quite persuasive. Because these monsters were illegals, Vinny was not bound by any rules to extract the information that they needed. Vinny's son, Dominic, was the football player & friend that caught Keri on the stairs the last time she fainted at school. For Vinny, this was personal.

"I will find out which one of these bastards killed Keri & then watch him be executed," thought Vinny.

Through evidence collected at the home, the agents learned the names of the other two illegals & that both were related to Luis Cortes; one was his brother Eduardo & one was his cousin Rodrigo. Vinny suspected that Luis was the mastermind. *"I just need to make these other two rats squeal,"* thought Vinny. He decided to start with his cousin Rodrigo.

The door to Rodrigo's cell was open & Vinny marched in. "Mr. Cortes, I am Vinny & I got a few questions for you."

"EAT SHIT & DIE GRINGO. I WON'T TALK," yelled Rodrigo. With one quick spin kick, Vinny's right foot caught on the left side of

Rodrigo's face – knocking out two front teeth.

Blood was now trickling from Rodrigo's mouth.

"Go to hell you bastard," screamed

Rodrigo as he tried to wipe the blood from his face.

Vinny grabbed Rodrigo's left arm,

dislocating his shoulder & broke his arm in two

places. "I can do this all day Cortes."

"Okay! Okay! What do you want to

know?" yelled Rodrigo.

"Who runs the narcs lab?" asked Vinny.

Rodrigo stared ahead & refused to say.

"I see," said Vinny. "So here's what's

going to happen. A young girl died because you

have a vendetta against our country. We think one

person made the call & only that person will get

capital punishment, but we need to know who it

was. Otherwise, we are prepared to execute all three

of you by lethal injection. So, if I were you, I would sing."

"It was Luis," said Rodrigo writhing in pain. Vinny got up & was about to walk out.

"What about my shoulder & arm?" cried Rodrigo.

"I will come back later with a doctor, but if you try any more shit, I will snap your neck like a twig, got it?" warned Vinny.

"Yes," murmured Rodrigo.

The guard opened the door, let Vinny out, & locked the cell door again.

The door to Eduardo's cell was open & Vinny walked in. "Mr. Cortes, I am Vinny & I got a few questions for you."

"GO FUCK YOURSELF WHITE DEVIL!" screamed Eduardo.

In the blink of an eye, Vinny landed multiple punches to Eduardo's chest – breaking several ribs.

'YOU MOTHERFUCKER!" yelled Eduardo.

Vinny then punched Eduardo's nose – breaking his nose. Blood was now running down Eduardo's chin. "You Cortes boys are a bunch of dumb asses, aren't you?" said Vinny.

"What're your questions?" asked Eduardo.

"Are there any others besides you three in the lab?" asked Vinny.

"Just us three," replied Eduardo.

"Who runs the narcs lab?" asked Vinny.

"I can't tell you. He will kill me!" exclaimed Eduardo.

"Like I just told one of your relatives, a young girl died because you have a vendetta against our country. We think one person made the call & only that person will get capital punishment, but we need to know who it was. Otherwise, we are prepared to execute all three of you by lethal injection. So, if I were you, I would talk."

"I won't die for him. Luis runs the show. You bastard!" cried Eduardo.

"See? You should have kept your mouth shut dickhead!" replied Vinny & landed a left-foot spin kick on Eduardo's right jaw – dislocating his jawbone.

Eduardo laid on the floor of his cell whimpering like a little child. Vinny walked out of Eduardo's cell & the jail cell was locked once more.

Vinny then went to see Luis. "You got some explaining to do Cortes," said Vinny.

"GO TO HELL GRINGO! I DON'T HAVE TO EXPLAIN SHIT TO YOU!" screamed Cortes.

"That's where you are wrong, you Panamanian turd," replied Vinny. With one hand on Luis' neck & one hand on Luis' crotch, Vinny picked up Luis over Vinny's head, spinning Luis in midair, & dropping Luis hard over a straight metal chair, breaking Luis' back.

"Help! Help! My back! I can't walk!" cried Luis.

"You killed our friend & now it's your turn," said Vinny. "Don't go away, I'll be right back."

"I can't fucking move," cried Luis now in excruciating pain.

Vinny went out to call his former Air Force superior.

"Hello?" asked the male voice on the phone.

"Yes Sir, I am looking for Colonel Benjamin Kemp," said Vinny.

"Yes, this is Ben."

"Hi Colonel Kemp, this is Captain Veragamo...now Special Agent Veragamo with the FBI."

"Hey Vinny. What can I do for you?" asked Ben.

"We got him, Sir. We got the bastard that is responsible for Keri's death," replied Vinny. "You want to exact your revenge?"

"I have an idea after seeing the autopsy. The piece of shit poisoned Keri but tried to cover his tracks. Let's meet at Weyler Lake after sentencing," said Ben.

"You got it," replied Vinny.

Vinny returned to Luis' cell. "Cortes, you really fucked up. The girl you killed was the colonel's daughter. Not only will you be sentenced to death, but you will also die a long, slow, excruciatingly painful death. You will be begging to die & death will not come fast enough for you. You go to hell you damn piece of shit."

Vinny told the guard outside "Get on the radio & get a stretcher. We'll have to get him in a hospital bed for some time until his execution."

After Vinny left, a stretcher was brought to lift up Luis & then transferred to a hospital bed inside his cell. Luis was placed in traction to try to immobilize his movement to avoid further back damage. Prison personnel checked on him every two to three hours; otherwise, Luis stared at the ceiling & questioned everything he had ever done. He began to bitterly weep. Later that night, Luis woke to the smell of brimstone & was terrified to see two shadows in his cell. He was paralyzed with fear.

"Damn Cortes. Looks like you ran your mouth one too many times, now you're stuck in this hospital bed with a broken back & a broken ass!" exclaimed Baal.

"You fool. You are no longer of use to me. Your foolish human pride has cost you dearly this time. Give me one good reason why I shouldn't kill you now," fumed Satan. "Your death will come after an extended period of great suffering – that should be ample training for the suffering you will face in hell. Your recklessness & stupidity have come back to bite you in the ass."

"Possess me! Let me get revenge on the man that did this to me!" exclaimed Luis.

"WE DON'T POSSESS FOOLS THAT GO & GET THEIR BACKS BROKEN. IT WOULD BE A COMPLETE WASTE OF MY TIME!" yelled Satan.

"If you want to see the man that did this to you, all you have to do is look in the mirror. You did it to yourself you idiotic moron," added Baal.

At that moment, both Satan & Baal departed from Luis' room.

The doorbell rang at the Kemp's home. Lois looked through the peephole & saw Susan standing outside. Lois opened the door & said "Hi Susan, we have been expecting you. Keri thought the world of you."

"M..m..m... Mrs. Kemp?" stuttered Susan.

"That's right Susan. Would you like to come inside?"

"Yes please Mrs. Kemp"

"Would you like to see Keri's room? We haven't been in there much since..."

"I would like that very much, thank you," replied Susan.

Lois thought that if she could get Susan one-on-one that Susan may talk. As they entered Keri's room upstairs, Lois let Susan look around & relax.

"She..sh.. she had a very nice room, but I came to see you for another reason," said Susan. "I have something to tell you; something you need to know."

"What is it?" asked Lois.

"Keri did not blindly go downtown looking for OxyContin 80. Someone at school gave her the drug dealer's phone number," answered Susan.

"Who was it?" inquired Lois.

"It was Vanessa, a former basketball teammate of Keri," replied Susan.

"I am calling the police. She needs to be brought in for questioning," said Lois.

"That is not possible Mrs. Kemp. Vanessa's mother found her this morning. Vanessa committed suicide last night. She left a note that she was overwhelmed with guilt & she feels responsible for Keri's death, but she never meant for it to happen. She was just trying to help Keri," stated Susan.

"That's terrible. Thank you for letting me know Susan," said Lois. "Perhaps one day we can make sense of all of this..."

"Yes Ma'am," replied Susan.

"So how are you doing Susan?" asked Lois.

"I um I uh," stammered Susan "I am homeless. Ever since my dad died & my mother was admitted to a mental hospital, I have been out on the street. Some nights, I have a bed at the homeless shelter. Otherwise, I try to sleep in the public library in an out-of-the-way spot. I go to school early to take a shower in the mornings."

"Susan, would you like to live with us? I am an attorney & can have the paperwork drawn up today. We would become your legal guardians," replied Lois.

"I uh I don't know," said Susan.

"Susan, I have been married to Benjamin Kemp for the last 20 years. He is a fine upstanding man; so you don't have to worry about him," stated Lois.

"Keri used to tell me how awesome of a mom & dad she had," replied Susan. For the first time in a long time, Susan felt tears in her eyes. "Oh Mrs. Kemp, I don't know what to say!"

"Say yes & then we can see about shopping a bit later today for any essentials that you may need," said Lois.

"Thank you Mrs. Kemp!" exclaimed Susan. Lois & Susan embraced, then Lois started making some calls to get the process started for legal guardianship.

After reviewing all of the evidence seized in the home of Luis Cortes, the Public Defender had no choice than to advise the Cortes men to plead guilty to all charges & throw themselves upon the mercy of the court. The District Attorney was pushing for the death penalty for Luis Cortes & a 25-year prison sentence for both Rodrigo Cortes & Eduardo Cortes; both were present in the courtroom during the trial. Luis Cortes was viewed in his jail cell lying in his hospital bed.

The jury unanimously voted guilty on all counts & supported the death penalty for Luis Cortes in the first-degree murder of Keri Kemp with the Kemp family electing to choose either lethal injection or the electric chair. After discussing among themselves, both Ben & Lois Kemp chose lethal injection for the execution of Luis Cortes. As of April 2019, the State lethal injection protocol called for a 3-drug combination, beginning with midazolam. However, through Ben's contacts in the Department of Defense (DoD), the Kemps were granted an exemption to determine an alternative combination of drugs inspired by some of the ingredients found in the Cortes lab – which was considered Confidential information & not shared with either the media or the public. All of Keri's friends were relieved that justice would be served &

the monster that killed their precious Keri would not

live to kill another human being. Her school

arranged a memorial plaque to be placed in the

hallway with a collection of photographs of Keri

with her many friends from different races &

religions indicative of Keri's pure heart & soul. To

witness the execution of her murderer would help

her friends take another step in their journey of

healing.

On the day of his execution, Luis Cortes

was allowed a final meal several hours before his

execution – which he struggled to eat because of his

nerves. His back had somewhat healed & he was no

longer in need of a hospital bed. He had been

transferred from the county jail to a state prison

weeks ago. A priest was brought to his cell & the

priest offered to perform the last rites as well as

pray for Cortes. Cortes cursed & yelled at the priest who abruptly left Cortes' cell.

"I worship Satan & Baal! Your God has never helped me!" screamed Cortes.

"That is not the way to address a man of God," said Vinny standing in the doorway of Luis Cortes' prison cell. Two prison guards handcuffed Cortes' hands behind his back & shackled his ankles.

"Gentlemen, please give us 30 minutes alone. I have a confidential message to give to Mr. Cortes," added Vinny. As the two guards made their way to the cell door, it was opened for them to pass through.

"Please don't leave me alone with him!" begged Luis Cortes. The two guards shook their heads as they walked out.

"See you in 30 minutes Vinny," said one of the guards.

Turning to Cortes, Vinny reached into his duffel bag & pulled out a taser.

"No! No! No!" cried Cortes.

Vinny let out a deep sigh. "YOU LITTLE PUNK ASS BITCH! YOU PICKED THE WRONG COUNTRY TO INVADE, THE WRONG GIRL TO KILL, & THE WRONG FAMILY TO CROSS!" yelled Vinny zapping Cortes with the taser.

"But I never met or saw the Kemp girl! I didn't know her!" exclaimed Cortes.

"Do you remember telling your accomplices that you referred to Keri as another white bitch & you wanted to kill as many white bastards as possible?" asked Vinny.

"I never said those things!" pleaded Cortes as Vinny zapped him again with the taser before screaming in pain.

"Really? In separate interrogations, your two accomplices corroborated each other's testimony," replied Vinny before zapping Cortes again with Cortes trembling in pain.

"Help me God!" begged Cortes.

"God won't help you now. Your last chance for God's help was the priest you just insulted," answered Vinny. Vinny put the taser back in his duffel bag & pulled out two brass knuckles fitting his fingers into both brass knuckles.

"What are you doing?" asked Cortes.

"Like I told the guards, I got a message to deliver from Keri's family, friends, teachers, coaches, classmates, & teammates," replied Vinny. Vinny started throwing punches with both hands as

Cortes absorbed punches to the face, neck, chest, stomach, back, & groin. Moments later, the cell door opened & the prison guards returned with wet cloths & towels. The prison guards wiped the sweat, blood, & dirt off of Cortes.

"It's time," said Vinny as the two guards escorted Cortes to the execution chamber of the prison. As they reached the execution chamber, a crowd of Keri's loved ones waited for the curtain to open to witness the execution of Luis Cortes. Cortes was forced to sit down & had both his arms & his legs strapped to the chair. Beside the chair was a small table with a silver tray containing a syringe full of the lethal injection. The execution chamber door swung open & in walked Retired Air Force Colonel Benjamin Kemp. Ben knelt beside Cortes' left ear & began to whisper.

"Okay, you Panamanian turd, we got a little surprise for you. Since you wanted to mix in extra ingredients into my baby's painkiller, we thought we would return the favor & we got clearance from the DoD - so it's legal," whispered Ben.

"What did you mix in it?" cried Cortes.

"In addition to 3-drug lethal injection protocol for this state, we have added spider venom from the black widow & the brown recluse, snake venom from the rattlesnake, water moccasin, copperhead & coral snake, the narcotics cocaine, heroin, & LSD. In addition, we have added both poisons arsenic & anthrax to maximize your suffering. May you rot in hell," whispered Ben.

Ben turned & walked out joining Lois, Susan & Vinny outside the execution chamber window. The executioner took the syringe in his hand & stuck Cortes in the neck, emptying the

entire contents into Cortes & then placing the empty

syringe back on the silver tray. Cortes writhed in

pain & let out bloodcurdling screams. He

hallucinated seeing all forms of monsters, demons,

wild animals, & interstellar aliens as indicated by

the look of absolute terror in his eyes.

"Die you motherfucker!" yelled Keri's

school classmates & friends.

"You're finally getting what you deserve,"

screamed Susan with tears running down her face.

"WE HOPE YOU ARE TORMENTED

FOREVER!" yelled Lois.

At last, Luis Cortes breathed his last breath

& was pronounced dead 45 minutes after receiving

the lethal injection.

Over the next several months, Susan became more & more comfortable in the Kemp home. She began to know & understand both Ben & Lois Kemp; appreciating that they had opened their home & their hearts to her. As a result of their care, guidance, & patience, Susan began to flourish & thrive in their nurturing home. She wrote an inspiring editorial to the local newspaper on Keri Kemp & her parents; it was so inspiring that the yearbook staff at her high school asked permission to use it as both a memorial to Keri & a tribute to her wonderful parents in their upcoming yearbook. The Keri Kemp Memorial Scholarship was created & funded by the Huntsville business community to be awarded each year to a deserving high school student that exemplified the values that endeared Keri to so many people. She may be gone, but her memory lived on the hearts & minds of her family,

her friends, & her community.

Chapter 6
Last Man on Earth

Ethan Mason was a shy, socially awkward high school sophomore in Memphis, TN. He always noticed the girls, but for the most part, they ignored him. Previously, he had gotten lots of friend requests on both Instagram & Twitter, but most of the kids had long moved on from Facebook as more and more adults had permeated it; so he rarely if ever logged on to it anymore. Most of the girls that sent him a friend requests only wanted him to like & share their photos or their comments; they could care less of having him as a flesh and blood friend. When he would post either photos or comments, they never liked or shared his comments. At the tender young age of 16, Ethan had figured out the game & didn't bother to even try to associate with most of the school kids as he chalked it up as a lost cause. *"I'll leave them alone & hopefully they will leave me alone,"* contemplated Ethan. *"Besides, someday I may be the CEO of a company & most of them may work for me. I'll show them."*

Many of the attractive girls wanted to become famous, either by becoming a singer, actress, or fashion model. While it is true that they were either very pretty or downright beautiful, most of them thought that they were God's gift to the human race & were not good, decent human beings. On the contrary, they were selfish, narcissistic, greedy, backstabbing bitches. Even though they did look good, they all had their issues & different forms of baggage that turned off most of their classmates, both guys & girls, because their classmates saw straight through the fancy clothes, hair, & make-up knowing how shallow & self-centered these girls had become. These attractive girls became so desperate for attention from their classmates (especially the boys) that they were blowing up their smartphones with their latest photos. Each time a new set of photos were posted on social media, most of the aspiring models would ask the same stupid questions. Every one of them wanting to know if they were the prettiest, hottest, & sexiest girl in the school.

Ranking anything less than the prettiest, hottest, & sexiest girl caused many of the girls to have a complete meltdown. While being ranked less than the absolute best bruised the egos of these narcissistic girls, Ethan had figured an even more effective way to humble these self-centered girls; he ignored them & it drove them absolutely insane! The more he ignored them, the more incensed they would become.

"How dare we be ignored! Doesn't everyone understand just how special we are?" complained these bitchy girls. Ethan, as well as others in the school, knew the moment that they gave these girls validation by liking, sharing, & replying to these girls' comments & photos, that these same girls would ghost them. These girls caused their own attention drought & further alienated most everyone in the school by their contemptuous behavior, princess attitude, & sense of entitlement. They couldn't comprehend why the whole city of Memphis; the whole state of Tennessee wasn't fawning over them. As time went on, these girls began to be resentful – especially towards their classmates, who in their feeble minds, had betrayed these girls. They became determined to make an example out of someone to send the message that they would no longer be ignored!

Several of these girls had noted that although they were connected with Ethan on social media, he never gave them feedback. They also noted that he was a loner & probably no one would stand up for him or even miss him should he suddenly get suspended from school for a week or two.

"Sisters, come over to my house tonight at 8:00 pm. We can talk downstairs in the game room. It's time that we make some noise," declared Ashley who the other girls considered their leader & she was the most outspoken of them all. She usually said what they were all thinking but didn't have the guts to say it. At 8:00 pm that night, Ashley welcomed Emma, Fran, Hannah, Isabel, Lisa, Michelle, Olivia, Sophia, & Tracy to the game room located in the basement of her family's home in Germantown – one of the more affluent areas around Memphis.

"Thank you all for coming," began Ashley. "These little people have ignored us for way too long. All of us have a chance to become highly successful fashion models & these rodents at our jerkwater school need a reminder of who is in charge of the student body. We are going to accuse Ethan Mason of trying to rape one of us down here in this room, but we will need to invite him here to put him at the scene of our little false rape allegation," Ashley laughed a sadistic laugh. *"We'll get that little fucker."* thought Ashley.

"Which one of us is going to play the victim?" asked Emma.

"I nominate Tracy – since she is the only one of us that has taken Drama courses. She has the best chance of convincing the police & the public that he did it," answered Ashley.

"Whoa! Wait! Hold it," replied Tracy. "I may not be attracted to the little creep, but I'm not trying to destroy his life. I am out of here," Tracy stood up to make her way to the stairs & leave.

"Sit down Tracy," demanded Ashley. "It would be most unfortunate if I showed your parents your nude photos that I pulled off of the Pink Meth site from a couple of years back. I know you only meant for your boyfriend at the time to see them. The internet is forever. Maybe the next time you get ready to do something that dumb again, you will pause & reconsider."

"YOU FUCKING BITCH!" screamed Tracy – throwing herself back down into the chair.

"You're right. I'm a fucking bitch & that's why I'm in charge of this little social club," exclaimed Ashley. "Somebody has to keep you pretty, stupid cunts in line – so might as well be me."

"Go to hell Ashley – we're not putting up with your shit anymore. We're all leaving," said Michelle.

"This is not a kidnapping – so I can't hold you all hostage. I just have dirt on all of you whores. Drinking problems, drug problems, abortions, STDs, cheating scandals at school," added Ashley. "I have enough to destroy all of you. A little trick I learned from a certain former First Lady – among other things. So, if you bitches don't mind, there are a few more details to hash out."

All of the other girls huffed & puffed but returned to their seats – glaring at Ashley like the deranged psycho that she was.

"My parents are out of town this coming weekend. We are going to have a little party &

invite a few loser boys, including Ethan Mason, that are not socially connected. We'll add some Rohypnol (a date rape drug) to his drink & while he's passed out, Tracy will take his semen, & his DNA to be used as evidence against him. He won't remember a thing & it will our word against his word," explained Ashley.

Most of the girls shook their heads, murmuring under their breaths, & thinking *"this is the worst idea that Ashley has ever concocted,"* but didn't dare cross her. *"The best thing for us is if Ashley got abducted, never to be seen or heard from again,"* pondered Emma.

Ashley sent an invitation to Ethan & a few other boys via DM. *"Hey guys, we are having a Getting-To-Know-You Party at my house Friday night from 8:00 pm – 1:00 am. Text me back & let me know. Thanx."*

"I can come. Please send me your

address," replied Ethan.

"Sweet! The address is 69 Kimbrough

Woods Place, Germantown, TN 38139," answered

Ashley. *"CU Friday night."*

"K," replied Ethan.

On Friday night, Ethan's older sister

Sarah offered to drop Ethan at Ashley's house not

only to get him there safely but also to try to talk

him out of going to the party at all.

"I got a bad feeling about this Ethan,"

explained Sarah. "I don't like it worth a damn!

These people won't even give you the time of day

& now all of a sudden they want to get you alone in

an unfamiliar place? I smell one big-ass rat little

brother." Ever since their parents were killed in a

car accident 3 years earlier, Sarah had assumed the

role of Ethan's caregiver. She was already grown &

had a lucrative career as a network systems engineer by the time her parents had passed away. Sarah could have been one of the world's greatest computer hackers had she so chosen, but instead, she turned her computer expertise into a very fulfilling career. She was able to provide Ethan with a very stable home.

"Do your sister a favor, I have some items that I want you to wear," said Sarah. "Don't worry, they're discreet."

"Really? You got to be kidding me!" exclaimed Ethan.

"Humor me Ethan. If I'm wrong, I'll admit it, but I sense something is bad wrong with this scenario," added Sarah.

Ethan hated to admit it, but Sarah was always discovering the latest technologies & through her work contacts, she had access to items that were typically only found in government capacities – some of the greatest new items for techies like him. Ethan let out a deep sigh & thought *"at least they won't be lame gadgets."*

"What items?" asked Ethan.

"First, this looks like a wearable bracelet, right? It's a voice recorder & a camera, but it also captures biometric vitals that you can easily display if someone should get suspicious. So, slip off your smartwatch & replace it with this bracelet," answered Sarah. "It is tamper-proof, so even if you're asleep, no one can remove it because I have the keys – one with me & one at home.

"Last, this looks like a normal necklace holding two medicine tablets & it displays the medical emergency logo, but like the bracelet it's also a voice recorder & a camera. Both devices are on a live feed," explained Sarah.

"You're going to be spying on ME?" exclaimed Ethan.

"No, not spying on you – spying on them," replied Sarah. "I'm chilling in Germantown & I'll be close by should you need me to pick you up early. I'm away from my hardware, so I've asked Megan, my trustworthy hacker friend, to just keep an eye on things. She's working on other projects too, but she will be recording both audio & video – just in case."

"Jeez! This is nuts!" replied Ethan.

"Don't be mad Ethan – it's only because I love you," said Sarah. "I've always had your back & always will."

"I love you too, but can you drop me at the corner? I'll text you when I'm ready to go home," added Ethan.

"No problem brother. One more thing, if they try to log onto the dark web, get the hell out of there. There are some really sick people on it & they can destroy your life before you figure out what's going on," added Sarah as she stopped at the corner near Ashley's house.

"Got it," answered Ethan as he opened the car door to get out. "See you."

"See you soon Ethan. Have fun," replied Sarah. Ethan nodded & walked down to Ashley's house. Once Sarah saw Ethan at Ashley's front door, she pulled away. Sarah immediately called Megan.

"Hey Sarah."

"Hi Meg. Please activate the live stream for both audio & video. Please merge them into a synchronized format & back up the files," requested

Sarah. "I have already sent your payment through Patreon. Thanks Meg."

"You got it, Sarah," replied Megan. "Thanks for the business." Sarah was one of Megan's favorite clients. Sarah paid well & was reasonable with her expectations.

The front door to Ashley's home opened & there Ethan was greeted by Ashley.

"Hi Ethan," exclaimed Ashley. She went to hug him ensuring that her right breast pressed against his chest. *"Let's see how thirsty this little punk is,"* thought Ashley - trying to turn Ethan on.

Ashley led Ethan downstairs to the basement game room. Ethan was relieved to see his Moroccan friend Amjad also in attendance as was Amjad relieved to see Ethan. Ethan had befriended Amjad at the beginning of the school year & they tried to stay in touch although they had no classes together this semester. Amjad's computer had previously stopped working & when Ethan told Sarah, she was able to take Amjad's computer to her workplace & completely upgraded Amjad's computer by replacing the power supply, hard drive, adding more memory & additional USB ports. She also helped Amjad set up a secure firewall. So, Amjad had learned to trust the Masons.

"Hi Amjad!" exclaimed Ethan extending his hand to shake.

"Hi Ethan. Good to see you," replied Amjad. "I'm not sure how long I'm staying. The computer is acting up again."

"I am sorry about that Amjad. You want to let Sarah work on it again?" asked Ethan.

"That's okay brother. I think it's the motherboard. If so, I'm just going to ask my family to purchase me a new computer," answered Amjad.

"Until then, Sarah fixed my Dell notebook & is running as well as my HP desktop. If you want to borrow the Dell until you get a new one, then it is yours to use, Amjad," said Ethan.

"Thank you, Ethan! That would be great! I've been using a computer at the library, but the library is kind of out of my way," replied Amjad.

"Awesome. If you can swing by this weekend, I will get you squared away," answered Ethan.

"Thanks brother," exclaimed Amjad. "*For all of the bad press about the Americans, I am still amazed at their generosity,*" thought Amjad.

"Okay, sissy boys! Time to get this party started," exclaimed Ashley. "What are you boys drinking tonight?"

"I think that is my queue to leave," said Amjad. "See you this weekend Ethan!" Amjad ran

as fast as he could up the stairs & out the door.
Once outside, Amjad texted his brother from the
street corner & his brother arrived moments later.

"Ethan, come sit in this wide easy chair!
It's very comfortable," blurted Tracy. *"It's easier to
mount an unsuspecting boy if he's in a wide chair,"*
thought Tracy.

"And what are you drinking Ethan?" asked
Ashley again.

"Well well, uh, I, uh..." stammered Ethan.

"I see, why don't we start you with a
smooth drink – say like a Canadian Mist & Sprite,"
suggested Ashley. Ashley mixed the drink for Ethan
while slyly adding Rohypnol to make Ethan more
compliant.

"So, Ethan what do you like best? Anal
sex, missionary sex, or oral sex?" asked Sophia –

throwing her head back laughing while Ashley handed Ethan his drink.

"Drink up Ethan! There is more where that came from," cried Ashley. "Most days we ignore little rodents like you & you would be the last man on earth that we would fuck, but we are feeling horny & want to give you a night you will never forget."

One of the girls started playing a metal music mix by Black Sabbath, Ozzy Osborne, Megadeath, & AC/DC. One by one, the girls started dancing in a large circle while throwing their clothes off as Ethan's eyes & the erection in his pants got bigger & bigger.

"It looks like our boy is a virgin," Sophia whispered to Tracy. "If you don't want to fuck him, I sure as hell will! I love to fuck virgin boys & feel that explosion, then I watch them follow me around – begging for more."

"Sorry Sophie," replied Tracy with a whisper. "That little boy is all mine!" Tracy & Sophie both laughed an evil laugh. By now, all of the girls were completely nude - dancing in a circle in the most provocative, seductive way possible. Ethan had drunk most of his drink & was feeling more than a bit drunk, but also drugged as his eyes became heavier & heavier as the Rohypnol took effect.

"WAKE UP ETHAN," screamed Sophia. "Have you ever seen so many nude dancing pussies in one place?" Then all of them laughed. By now, Ethan had completely finished his drink & was completely unconscious although his penis was still extremely erect.

"Remove his shoes, pants, & underwear only. We need to do this quickly in case he somehow wakes up while Tracy is on him," commanded Ashley.

Tracy mounted on top of Ethan & guided his penis inside her vagina. Then Tracy copulated Ethan as hard & fast as she could until she felt him ejaculate inside her while he remained unconscious. "Mmmm! That felt SOOO good," moaned Tracy. "That was yummy!"

She used both hands to scratch into Ethan's sides, arms, hands & neck to show a struggle. Tracy then told the girls to slap her, punch her & kick her to show signs of physical abuse. Ashley told Tracy to cower in the corner, & curl into a fetal position. They squirted lots of eye drops into Tracy's eyes & while Ethan remained unconscious, Tracy called 911 to report that she had been raped. All of the

girls quickly dressed & most of them quietly waited
in Ashley's bedroom on the 2nd floor of the house
for the police to arrive & leave. Germantown police
arrived & moments later, Ethan regained
consciousness & was immediately arrested for
raping Tracy.

A rape counselor arrived & took an
extremely distraught & shattered Tracy to the
hospital to let doctors use a rape kit on Tracy. Tracy
tried her best to sell the lie & continued to cry,
shake, & mumble. The rape counselor brought
Tracy back to Ashley's house because Tracy
"wanted to be with her sisters during this horrible
time." After the rape counselor left, the girls let out
unbridled laughter. They washed all of the drink
glasses, cleaned up the game room, & wiped it
down to remove all evidence.

Sophia had shot a video of Ethan Mason being handcuffed & taken into custody by the Germantown Police. She made sure to capture the despair, disbelief, & fear in Ethan's eyes & the tears running down his face. Ashley edited the video to add an audio commentary without showing her face.

"Listen up, you little pricks. Observe the despondency of one Ethan Mason on this video. This is our warning shot. You little shits better stop ignoring us & give us the props that we deserve, or you will be the next Ethan Mason," demanded Ashley. She then uploaded the edited video & they posted the video on both Instagram & Twitter. The girls then pulled back the large rectangular rug from the game room floor to fully display their Satanic pentagram. The girls, all now dressed in black robes with red hoods held hands in a circle around the pentagram & prayed to Satan & his demons. They pledged their souls in exchange for successful

fashion modeling. At the end of their Satanic

prayers, they adjourned, changed back into their

street clothes & called it a night.

      The police officers roughly pushed Ethan

into an interrogation room – unaware that both the

necklace & the bracelet were still recording both

audio & video.

      "Why did you rape that young lady?"

grilled Sergeant Anderson.

      "I didn't rape anybody. I was drugged &

the next thing I remember was you two officers

standing over me to arrest me," replied Ethan.

      "Listen, you little piece of shit. The rape

test confirmed both your semen & your DNA were

inside Tracy's vagina. You really have no defense,"

said Sergeant Fuller. "Tracy is my best friend's

daughter."

"None of this makes any sense. I am not a rapist," cried Ethan.

"Tell it to the judge, you rat bastard!" yelled said Sergeant Fuller.

Ethan was taken to the general holding cell for new arrests. Ethan was born with an undetected defect in his heart & due to the anxiety & the stress of his situation, Ethan had a massive heart attack overnight & died in his sleep. The next morning, fellow inmates screamed for help & once an officer saw that Ethan had died, his body was sent to the morgue.

The next morning, Megan noticed that Ethan's live feed had stopped, but because she had fallen asleep while Ethan was still sipping a drink in his chair, Megan was unaware of everything that had transpired. She played back the entire audio/video file – in shock from everything that she had witnessed up until Ethan was placed in the general holding cell. Megan immediately called Sarah – who had fallen asleep in her car while waiting to pick up Ethan from the previous night. Sarah jumped from the sound of her ringing phone.

"Hi Sarah, something happened to Ethan last night. Can you come to my house? I will show you everything captured on audio/video," said Megan.

"On the way Megan," replied Sarah.

After reviewing the entire recording with Megan, Sarah sat in disbelief – too upset to move. "These fucking cunts drugged & raped my little brother, & then had him arrested on some false rape allegation," said Sarah.

"That would be the gist of it," replied Megan.

"I'm going down to the police station to get him out of jail, then I am going to ask my attorney to meet us at home this afternoon," stated Sarah. "Megan please make sure that the file is sent to both my computer, Ethan's computers, & please archive a back-up."

Sarah reached the Germantown police station & ran inside to get Ethan released. *"I knew something was not quite right with this whole party deal,"* worried Sarah. Upon reaching the main information desk of the police department, Sarah asked to see Ethan Mason. The officer picked up his phone & called the police chief to the desk.

"Miss Mason, I am Police Chief Morgan. Please come with me."

"Where is my brother."

"He is in this room," replied Chief Morgan.

"But that room is the morgue," said Sarah with tears in her eyes.

Chief Morgan opened a storage door & pulled the tray out with Ethan's body laid upon it. She gasped in disbelief.

"ETHAN! NO! NO! NO," screamed Sarah. "WHY? WHY HIM?"

"He had a massive heart attack last night in his sleep," replied Chief Morgan. "I'm very sorry for your loss."

"He never should have been here, to begin with," exclaimed Sarah. "He was framed!"

"Miss Mason, we have evidence to suggest that he was guilty of..." said Chief Morgan.

"Well, you didn't have the most important evidence & now because of the GROSS INCOMPETENCE of your police department, my brother is dead," exclaimed Sarah. "You will be hearing from my attorney."

Through a fog of tears, Sarah drove back to Megan's home & when Megan opened the door, Sarah fell into Megan's arms sobbing uncontrollably & cried "Ethan's dead, Ethan's dead, Ethan's dead..."

"How?" asked Megan as the tears welled up in her eyes.

"Ethan had a massive heart attack in his shared jail cell last night," sobbed Sarah. "Would you please come to my home & vouch for me when my attorney comes over this afternoon?"

"Absolutely," said Megan hugging Sarah. "I'm here for you."

Sarah called Giles Harper, her personal attorney, to schedule a meeting for that afternoon.

"Giles, I'm sorry to call you on the weekend, but this can't wait until Monday," explained Sarah.

"I'll be there at 1:30 pm Sarah," replied Giles.

After reviewing the file with Sarah & Megan, Giles was clearly shaken by the news of Ethan's passing & was equally incensed at the heinous crime & cover-up perpetrated by these evil girls.

"Where are the two cameras that Ethan was wearing?" asked Giles.

"They are still on Ethan," replied Sarah.

"Sarah, I'm sorry, but we must have those cameras. Please go back to the morgue to get them. Perhaps there is additional recorded footage that was not transmitted back to Megan," explained

Giles. "Once you get them, let Megan see if there is more footage to discover."

"Megan, here is my email address. Please send me the entire audio/video file ASAP as well as any additional footage that you may discover," said Giles.

Sarah & Megan returned to the morgue & the attending officer allowed her to remove both the bracelet & necklace from her brother's body. Upon reaching Megan's home, Sarah turned both cameras over to Megan to research.

"I'm sorry to tie you up with this burden," cried Sarah.

"Sarah, I'm glad to help. I'll give it my utmost attention & top priority," replied Megan.

Within the next hour, Megan sent additional files to both Sarah & Giles – not only from Ethan's two cameras, but she had also hacked

into the security system at Ashley's home &
recovered everything that transpired *after the police
had left including the Satanic prayers & chants!*

"Bingo," said Giles after reviewing the
additional footage & he immediately called Sarah.

"During the police interrogation video
captured by Ethan's camera, he said he thought he
had been drugged. Sarah, I'm sorry to ask you this,
but may we have the coroner to do an autopsy on
Ethan? If he was in fact drugged with Rohypnol or
another date-rape drug, we can build even stronger
cases – both civil & criminal. All of these girls at
the party have a significant social media presence &
all of them belong to affluent members of
Germantown's High Society. I am almost certain
that the families will want this to go away as
quickly & quietly as possible," explained Giles.

"If the autopsy findings help you do your job, then do it, Giles" replied Sarah.

Sarah's doorbell rang & she saw that it was Ethan's friend Amjad. Amjad noticed that Sarah was crying – he did not know about Ethan's passing. Sarah embraced Amjad in an emotional way when seeking comfort for a tremendous loss.

"What's wrong Sarah?" inquired Amjad.

"Ethan had a massive heart attack & died last night," replied Sarah. Amjad fell in a chair out of disbelief & shock – his eyes filling with tears for his good friend as he stared at the floor.

"I can't believe it," said Amjad. "I saw him for a short time last night at the party & I left when the girls started bringing out the alcohol. I only stopped by today because my computer crashed again & Ethan offered to let me use his Dell notebook until my parents send me money for a new one."

"Sarah, I'm so sorry for your loss. I loved Ethan like a brother. He was so kind to me when I first came to America & we have been friends ever since," stated Amjad. "How is it possible that he had a massive heart attack? He was only 16 years old! What kind of anxiety & stress could have caused this tragedy?"

"Yes, we saw you on the video from the cameras that Ethan was wearing & we saw you leave early from the party," replied Sarah. "I wish to God that Ethan had left early too. I have something to show you Amjad. Please follow me," requested Sarah. Sarah played all of the audio/video files from Ethan's cameras both from Ashley's home & the clips from the police station. She also played for him the audio/video files that Megan captured from Ashley's home security system.

"THOSE EVIL WHORES," screamed Amjad. "They raped him while he had asleep & then accused him of rape, had him arrested & harassed by those two cops. No wonder Ethan was under such anxiety & stress!"

Sarah's doorbell rang & when she answered, Megan had dropped by to check on Sarah. Sarah introduced Megan to Amjad.

"I am sorry to meet you under such circumstances Amjad," said Megan. "Sarah speaks very highly of you. Ethan was a good guy."

"Amjad, Ethan would have wanted you to have his computers – both his HP desktop & his Dell notebook. So they are yours to take home with you. Megan, would you mind copying all of the files from both of Ethan's computers & send them to my computer? I think there may be more to all of this than we realize," said Sarah.

"Thank you Sarah," replied Amjad. "Once Megan is finished with them, I would be proud to take them."

"Amjad, if you run into any issues, here is my card," said Megan as she extended one of her business cards to Amjad. "If you like, I can follow you home & help you set up your hardware."

"Thank you, Megan," said Amjad. "That would be great."

"Amjad, in the meantime my attorney Giles is currently planning to file both civil & criminal charges against these girls," said Sarah. "May I give him your contact information should he have any questions?"

"By all means, Sarah," replied Amjad. "Ethan was my brother & you're my sister – so I'm ready to help bring them to justice in any way I can."

"Good. I will send it to him now," answered Sarah.

"Sarah, all files from both computers have been copied & transmitted to your computer," declared Megan. "So, Ethan's computers can be shut down & all cables disconnected."

"I can take the notebook now & come back later for the desktop, monitor, & peripherals. My car trunk is full & I need to empty it out," said Amjad.

"No worries Amjad. It can all go in the back of my SUV. I got you covered," replied Megan.

Several hours later after Megan had connected all of the hardware at Amjad's apartment,

Amjad offered Megan a cup of tea & a platter of samosas as he observed daily tea time.

"Megan, I know Sarah's attorney is working on bringing civil & criminal charges against those evil girls, but I'm consumed with rage against them. I think of Ethan & what those evil girls did to him. It's not so much seeking revenge against them, but of them coming face to face with the evil that they have done. They need a day of reckoning like a cold slap in the face," declared Amjad.

"I personally find women like that repulsive & they give all of us Western women a bad name," replied Megan. "Amjad, I hope that you know that women like Sarah & myself are not like them."

"I realize that Megan," said Amjad.

"Amjad, I agree with you though," said Megan. "Sarah is so inconsolable over the loss of Ethan & she feels guilty for letting him go to the party at all. I don't want these bitches to ever do this to another human being. No amount of punishment would be too great for them."

"Do you mean it Megan? Is that your true wish?" asked Amjad. "We both saw just how sadistic, perverted, & evil that they are. We can use their narcissism, & self-centered nature against them. We can pose as a fashion modeling agency to lure them to Europe or the Middle East & then find the highest bidder on the dark web; although the dark web does concern me. They would dearly pay for their transgressions & never do this evil to another boy."

"I'm in. Don't worry about the dark web. Being the sophisticated hacker that I am, I know some tricks to keep you safe & anonymous. Normally, I wouldn't be onboard for human trafficking, but under the circumstances, I've got no problem with it," exclaimed Megan. "I recommend at this point, we tell no one else. We may eventually tell Sarah, but now is not the time."

"The girls shared hundreds of modeling photos on Instagram & Twitter. Ethan never commented on them, but unbeknownst to them, Sarah, or me, he actually kept a folder of each girl's very best poses on his desktop computer. We can use these photos to initiate contact with each of them. It shouldn't be a problem to convince the girls that their airfare & accommodations will be provided," added Megan.

Ashley, Emma, Fran, Hannah, Isabel, Lisa, Michelle, Olivia, Sophia, & Tracy each received the following FedEx Overnight letter from

A+ Models, Milan, Italy addressed to each specific girl:

"Dear Future Supermodel, we have reviewed your very impressive portfolio & we have multiple clients in Milan & other locales that very much wish to meet you in person. We have extended this invitation to the other beautiful ladies in your area & have found traveling on such a long journey is less stressful if one is able to travel with their peers. We understand that your school is on Christmas Holiday from Friday, 18Dec2020 to Monday, 04Jan2021. Please find enclosed your round-trip airline tickets to & from Milan, Italy (2 stops: Chicago & Madrid). Kindly advise if you are unable to attend as we have other ladies interested in this golden opportunity. Best regards, A+ Models, Milan, Italy"

As each girl read the letter, they were extremely ecstatic & were blowing up each other's phones.

"OMG! OMG! It's finally happening next week! Goodbye hick town Memphis & Hello Milan!" exclaimed Ashley.

Later that week, their parents dropped them at the Memphis Airport – giving them a tearful goodbye but giving them wings to fly. After arriving & departing from Chicago's O'Hare Airport, they arrived for their next stop in Madrid, Spain. Upon arriving in Madrid, the ticketing agent found an update for each of the girl's tickets & the girls were ushered from the main Madrid Airport to the Executive Business Park where they boarded a Lear Jet – normally reserved for VIPs on Business Travel.

As the girls relaxed on the private jet, they were offered glasses on champagne laced with Rohypnol. The girls were all getting sleepy – thinking that both the jet lag & the fatigue were creeping upon them. Within moments, all 10 girls were unconscious. The jet landed in Minsk, Belarus & the girls were taken to a warehouse on the outskirts of town. They had all of their belongings taken away. Their smartphones, their passports, & their identifications were all destroyed. They woke up on the floor of the warehouse with their hands & feet bound with rope. Their mouths were gagged with handkerchiefs & they were alone in a foreign land. They struggled to scream & struggled to move – only to discover that they had been silenced. They saw men speaking a foreign language in the distance. One of the men approached them & spoke English with a strong accent.

"Well, what have we here? A herd of American sluts," exclaimed the Belarusian man. "Don't get too comfortable here because you may or may not remain in this country! Your smartphones, passports, & identifications have all been destroyed! We have seen all of the audio/video files leading up to your rape of Ethan Mason – who later that same night died in his jail cell of a massive heart attack. Your disgusting nude dancing, Satanic prayers & worship, filming of this boy's arrest, your false filing of a police report, & evil plan to frame this boy have been shared with the authorities back in America & will be shared with all of your families as well.

We own you as the glorified pieces of meat that you have chosen to become! You are all going to market – as in sold to the highest bidder! You better hope that you know how to please a man or group of men. You are no longer in the Progressive West! Speak only when spoken to & if you try to challenge a man, it could cost you your life! You have been warned! Pray that your life will be short & you can escape your hell on earth!"

One by one, the girls were helped to stand & had the handkerchiefs pulled down from their mouths; in disbelief & shock by what they had just heard. One by one, the girls glared at Ashley with disgust & contempt for leading them to such a horrific ending. They all felt stupid & embarrassed for being so gullible as to behave so recklessly in traveling far from home without protection & security. They all felt thoroughly ashamed.

Once the handkerchief was removed from her mouth, Ashley immediately began screaming for help & was shot in the head from close range – falling to the ground dead. All of the girls tried to suppress their screams & were reduced to whimpers & tears. One by one the girls were hauled off to be sold – never to be seen or heard from again.

Giles received the results of Ethan's autopsy from the coroner's office. The presence of Rohypnol was detected in Ethan's body; proof positive that Ethan had been drugged. Giles informed Sarah & updated the documentation for both the civil & criminal cases. Giles then called Judge Thomas Miller's office.

Judge Miller agreed to meet at Giles Harper's office given the amount of evidence that Giles needed to show to Judge Miller. Giles also presented Judge Miller with Ethan Mason's autopsy report. After reviewing all of the footage & the autopsy report, Judge Miller slowly sat down & murmured to himself staring down out the floor.

"Holy Mary Mother of God," thought Judge Miller – clearly shaken by what he had just observed.

"In my 40-plus years in the judicial system, I have never seen such an evil group of young ladies. This is truly shocking. Because of the disturbing behavior of Sergeants Anderson & Fuller, I will recommend to the Mayor that he demands Police Chief Morgan to launch an Internal Affairs Investigation to get to the bottom of this heinous crime; not only for the actions of the police but also for the rape counselor failing to follow protocol," declared Judge Miller. "They condoned the actions of these ladies & denied an innocent young man the right to be treated fairly & with dignity.

"Mr. Harper, consult with your client to find out what she is financially seeking in the civil suit. I know the families of most of these young ladies. They will be highly motivated to settle out of court. The last thing they want is for the civil suit tried in a public setting under the harsh scrutiny of the media – which could expand from local media to national media.

"For the criminal suit, clearly both the young lady that was the hostess of the party, as well as the young lady that raped Ethan Mason, would most likely be charged with involuntary manslaughter. The other young ladies would be charged as accomplices to involuntary manslaughter.

"2nd-degree murder is not a viable avenue because even though the ladies committed a heinous act against Ethan Mason, there is no evidence to suggest that they ever actually intended for the young man to die."

"Judge, if possible I need the audio/video footage for the entire evening of the party from the security company. Would you sign off on a subpoena if the security company refuses to supply me with the footage?" asked Giles.

"Absolutely Mr. Harper," replied Judge Miller. "In fact, make sure that when you send the demand for the footage to the security company that I am on the courtesy copy. State that if they fail to produce the footage that they will receive a subpoena that will come directly from me to appear in court!"

The security company sent the footage both electronically & video disc to Giles the same day that they received the request. Now Giles had all of the evidence that he needed to proceed with both the criminal trial & the civil trial.

Giles went to see Sarah in-person &
shared with her the judge's sentiments that revolved
around Ethan's death. Point blank, Giles asked
Sarah what financial compensation she was looking
for.

"Giles, that doesn't matter to me," replied
Sarah. "I just want justice to be served & I want
Ethan's good name to be cleared of any
wrongdoing."

The families of each of the 10 girls were
called into the judge's chamber one family at a time
& presented with all of the evidence that had been
collected from: the beginning of the party, the rape
of Ethan Mason, the Satanic dance & ritual
performed in the game room, to Ethan's
mistreatment in the police interrogation room, &
ending with the discovery of Ethan's dead body the
morning after the party. Giles was present with

Judge Miller as each family learned the darkest secrets of the daughters. The families were devastated at all that had transpired.

As predicted, each family was eager to settle out of court the civil suit to make the entire episode go quietly away. Through negotiations & signed letters of nondisclosure agreements, Giles was able to obtain a joint settlement from all 10 families for $50,000,000.00 awarded to Sarah Mason. In desperate need of a change of scenery, Sarah resigned from her job & moved back to her hometown of Erie, Pennsylvania. Her dear brother Ethan was laid to rest near his parents at a memorial garden in Erie.

When informed of the criminal charges that faced their respective daughters, the families informed both Judge Miller & Giles Harper that their daughters had gone to Europe for a modeling opportunity. The police issued arrest warrants for all 10 girls that would be served upon the girls' return to Memphis. At the end of December, Judge Miller's office received a large padded envelope from The Embassy of the United States, Minsk, Belarus.

Inside the padded envelope were both video discs & a brief note which stated, *"Please call in Giles Harper to view this video together, Signed, your friend from Belarus,"* Upon receiving the call from Judge Miller, Giles arrived shortly thereafter to Judge Miller's chambers.

"What is on this disc?" asked Giles – obviously having his curiosity piqued.

"I'm not sure," replied Judge Miller. "Whoever sent it wanted us to both see it together." Judge Miller closed the door to his chambers with only himself & Giles present. Judge Miller began playing the video – which started with the girls

arriving in Madrid, Spain & they were unknowingly

being filmed from afar being taken from the main

Madrid airport to the Executive Business Park. The

girls were filmed entering the Lear jet & sipping

champagne, falling asleep on the jet, & then waking

up on the floor of a warehouse in a foreign country.

The video captured the Belarusian man addressing

the girls, the murder of Ashley, & the abduction &

human trafficking of the remaining 9 girls.

"This is a nightmare that just will not end,"

sighed Judge Miller. "We need to inform their

parents. Mr. Harper, are you able to remain with me

while we pass along this most unfortunate turn of

events?"

"Yes Sir Judge. This is a burden too big

for one man to shoulder," replied Giles.

As each family was again called in one by one, they expected the worst & hoped for the best. Ashley's family witnessed via the video footage of the horrific fate that befell her. The other families became hysterical & were completely lost as to what to do next. They all reached out to the U.S. Embassy in Minsk, Belarus, but were dissuaded from going to Belarus as the families of the girls would also be at risk of being abducted. The families tried to remain hopeful of the return of their girls, but as time went on their hopes began to fade. The 10 Germantown girls who had such promising futures were lost forever.

Chapter 7
Deliver Us from Evil

Decades ago, both the Bloods & the Crips had some gang members move from Los Angeles, CA to St. Louis County, MO in the old Wellston & Pine Lawn hoods – away from the downtown St. Louis area. Both hoods were connected by Kienlen Avenue which had seen its fair share of gangland violence. Any attempts to call a truce between the Bloods & the Crips always seemed to be short-lived. Law enforcement struggled to understand if the rise in gangland violence was dictated by either local gang leaders or from the top gang leaders in Los Angeles. Both gangs ferociously defended their respective turfs & anyone that happened to aimlessly wander on the turfs of either gang found themselves in a world of hurt. Some victims were beaten, robbed, raped, or killed; only the most skilled negotiators escaped from gang turfs

unscathed & only then by paying a "turf toll."

Police were apprehensive to get involved as

previous attempts to break up gang violence ended

in more police fatalities & injuries while failing to

decrease the violence. They primarily got involved

while trying to rescue innocent bystanders. Every

day, the local hospital ER staff held their collective

breaths wondering how many of the injured, either

victims or gang members, would be brought in with

life-threatening injuries. Recent spikes in gangland

violence had drawn some unwanted attention to

both the Bloods & the Crips.

"If these foolish humans want to spill

blood & prove how evil they are, we are more than

willing to wipe out all of them," exclaimed Malphas

a demon superior with many legions of demons

under his command. "Since they think they the worst humans to ever walk the face of the earth, we will take them back in time & show them some of the evilest humans to have ever live."

Early one night, two full-size sedans raced along the north of Kienlen Avenue, then turned left on St. Louis Avenue while gunfire was exchanged between the occupants of the two cars. They both stopped near the barricaded entrance of St Peters Cemetery & they both ran into the open area of the cemetery. As they both took cover, they reloaded their automatic weapons to continue their assaults. Malphas & one of his legions appeared between the two gangs as dark, mysterious specters terrifying members of both gangs. The gangs tried to shoot the specters, but as the gangsters pulled the triggers all of the guns jammed & began to heat so hot that the guns burned their hands & all of the guns were dropped. The gangsters froze in fear. The demons overpowered the gang members pinning them against the trees' trunks.

"I am Malphas the demon superior who commands this & many other legions," stated Malphas. "Who are you?"

"We are the Bloods," said the gang to the left.

"We are the Crips," said the gang to the right.

"We are here to take you, boys, on a little trip in time," replied Malphas.

"DON'T CALL US BOYS YOU BASTARD!" yelled Dre, the leader of the Bloods who broke free from the demon's grip & tried to push Malphas from the side. Malphas did not budge.

Malphas turned, grabbing Dre by the neck with both hands, & snapped Dre's neck with both hands. "My mistake," replied Malphas as Dre's lifeless body fell to the ground.

"We are here to take you, GIRLS, on a little trip in time," said Malphas in a snarky tone.

"MOTHERFUCKER, YOU CAN'T TALK TO US LIKE THAT," screamed Mario, the leader of the Crips who was still in the grip of a demon.

"I can & I will talk to you in any manner I see fit," answered Malphas.

"YOU JUST DON'T GET IT, BITCH! THIS IS OUR TOWN," yelled Mario – now visibly shaken but trying to show his gang a sense of false bravado. "WE WILL RISE UP ON YOUR PUNK ASS!"

"This town no longer belongs to you," replied Malphas. "But you are right, you should rise up to new heights & I am just the demon superior to help you do just that."

"Bring the talking rodent to me," commanded Malphas to the demon holding Mario. Malphas grabbed Mario under both arms & flew straight up 36,000 feet holding Mario in place at that altitude until Mario froze to death. Malphas flew back down to the cemetery & throwing Mario's frozen body to the ground.

"Do any of you other human maggots have anything to say?" asked Malphas. Malphas read the minds of the remaining gang members in the cemetery to learn the locations of any other Bloods & Crips in St. Louis. Malphas directed some of his legions to collect the other gang members & forced them to the cemetery.

With every remaining gang member of both the Bloods & Crips, Malphas and his legion of demons teleported the Bloods & the Crips to Mongolia in the year 1220.

Genghis Khan conquered the majority of China & all of the land through the Caspian Sea. The gang members witnessed Khan's destruction of entire cities – killing soldiers, civilians, & children alike. They saw him kill people by pouring molten metal & silver in their eyes & ears – which made them nauseated. Gang members attested to the massacre of hundreds of thousands of people & the lowly were decapitated. They saw women raped in front of their families. Tens of thousands of people were enslaved. Many of the gang members shook their heads in disbelief with tears in their eyes.

"Malphas please," pleaded the Bloods'
gang member Raymond. "We have seen enough of
this evil bastard!"

"Very well," replied Malphas. "How many
people have your two gangs killed together in your
city of St. Louis?"

"Almost 200 for us Bloods," replied
Raymond.

"About the same for us Crips," answered
Curtis. Raymond locked eyes with Curtis as they
both were in shock & deeply shaken by what they
had just witnessed. Both kept shaking their heads as
they wiped the tears from their eyes.

"Genghis Khan & his army killed
between 20 to 60 million people," added Malphas.
"Looks like you won't be matching his record. Now
for our next stop in Wallachia, Romania in the year
1448 & a nickname you punks may recognize…

Vlad the Impaler… more commonly known in your history books as Vlad Dracula." Several of the gang members began to panic & several fell to their knees begging for the tour to end.

"Stop?" exclaimed Malphas. "Oh no boys! We're just getting started!"

"You got to be fucking kidding me," replied Raymond. "We are supposed to believe in the vampire Count Dracula? Are you out of your mind?" Raymond was trying to hold it together, but secretly he didn't know how much more of this he could take. Malphas laughed a sinister laugh.

"Vampire? Whether or not Vlad Dracula was an actual vampire is up to debate, but the legends do promote tourism for the people of Romania – especially from Wallachia to the Carpathian Mountains in northeastern Romania. The factual history of Vlad Dracula the man is even

more disturbing than the folk legend of Vlad
Dracula the vampire."

Vlad Dracula reigned on three different
occasions as the Prince of Wallachia. Both the
Bloods & the Crips were appalled & disgusted by
the sick, twisted, & repulsive actions of Vlad
Dracula. Never had they seen this level of evil
where people were tortured & slowly killed through
impalement from the rectum through the mouth.
Never had they witnessed the extended suffering of
some people taking days to die a cruel, painful
death. Never had they viewed innocent animals
treated in such an inhumane manner as they too
were impaled by Dracula. Never in their most
devious plans would they have ever massacred all
of the inhabitants of a town – killing everyone.
Men, women, & children were all murdered in the
city of Amlas – which became a ghost town to this

day. Villages that were simply on Vlad's march to war were destroyed out of hatred & spite. He murdered his own wife. He attracted the poor & the sick with a fake party & then had them all burned to death.

Of all of the evil that they witnessed at the hands of Vlad Dracula, the Bloods & the Crips were most disturbed by the murdering of children & babies. Vlad Dracula was so utterly evil that he forced the parents to eat their cooked children! After witnessing such horrors, the gangs pleaded with Malphas to move on from this most horrific scene.

"Vlad Dracula killed over 100,000 humans – most in a slow, painful death," added Malphas. "His evil rivals that of some of the evilest demons in hell. Our next stop on this tour of evil will be more recent as within the last 100 years. We

are now going to stop in Berlin, Germany in 1939."

The Bloods & the Crips attested to the

insanity of Adolf Hitler. As dictator of Nazi

Germany, he initiated World War II in Europe with

the invasion of Poland in September 1939. He

believed that Jews were the cause of all of

Germany's problems & considered them to be sub-

human. He planned to kill every Jew in Europe &

gain control of the world. The gang members

witnessed wounded people in hospitals used as lab

rats to test ways of killing with carbon dioxide gas –

which resulted in the death of over 300,000 people.

Every Jew in Germany eventually was taken to

concentration camps. Many from other countries

were also forced to concentration camps. Hitler

demanded all Jews to work until they died or were

killed. The Bloods & the Crips confirmed that millions of Jews were forced to watch friends and family members die. Jews were killed from gas chambers, crematories, firing squads, lethal injections, force labor, starvation, poison, exposure, disease, execution, death marches and medical experiments. This evil psychopath was responsible for the death of millions of children.

The gang members saw first-hand the piles of dead people stacked up at the death camps of the Nazis & were shocked beyond belief. They saw Jews in the concentration camps that were so malnourished that many could not stand by themselves. The Bloods & the Crips observed piles of shoes, piles of women's purses, & piles of eyeglasses. They smelled the burning of human corpses. They witnessed firing squads killing scores of people who fell into mass graves. *"Dear God in*

Heaven," thought Curtis as the gang members attested to such an overwhelming display of human suffering & tragedy. The Bloods & the Crips could not look anymore & prayed that they would be delivered from this evil.

"Adolf Hitler, Heinrich Himmler, Adolf Eichmann, Reinhard Heydrich, Josef Mengele, & many other Nazis were responsible for the deaths of over 50 million people," said Malphas.

"Oh my God!" cried Curtis.

"Indeed," replied Malphas. "Our next stop will be---"

"Please Malphas! No more!" pleaded Raymond.

"You've proved your point! Please! We've seen enough!" begged Curtis.

"You little talking maggots aren't near as bad as you thought you were before this show & tell," declared Malphas. "We were just about to go to Moscow, Russia 1940s to spend some quality time with another human scum named Joseph Stalin. He killed friends & foes alike. He also had people tortured, raped, & killed. At the end of World War II, his Red Army raped between 1.5 to 2 million German women since most of the German men had either been killed or captured – so they were not there to protect their women. About 10 percent of the German women raped died – most from suicide. When it was all said & done, Stalin was responsible for the deaths of 20 to 60 million people."

"There was also Pol Pot the Prime Minister of Cambodia, Idi Amin the dictator of Uganda, Ivan the Terrible the Tsar of Russia, Mao

Zedong the dictator of China, Emperor Hirohito of Japan, & so many others that were the evilest people that ever lived. And here you are with your little gangs – thinking that you are all that. You would be thrashed like wheat by any of these people," continued Malphas.

"Malphas, please take us back to St. Louis," begged Raymond.

"Please Malphas," pleaded Curtis.

"As I already stated, St. Louis is no longer your town, no longer your concern," answered Malphas. "You are guilty of the beating, robbing, raping, & killing of others. You will be judged in this life & the afterlife."

"We demand our attorneys be present! We demand a fair trial!" exclaimed Raymond.

"We demand justice be served!" added Curtis.

Malphas grabbed both Raymond & Curtis by the heads & headbutted them together – sending both gang members sprawling out of control on the ground.

"None of you are in a position to demand anything. You will have no defense present," replied Malphas. "But you will find the judges to be most fair & without prejudice. It is time for your judgment."

"Please wait Malphas," pleaded Raymond. "If we're not going back to St. Louis, then where are we going?"

"Yeah, where are we going?" echoed Curtis as he shuddered to think what was coming. Malphas sensed the terror that was now running through the minds of both the Bloods & the Crips.

"You should be scared," answered Malphas. "We are going to a place you have never been to before. To a harsh location in the Southern Hemisphere; one that separates the men from the boys." Malphas & his demons teleported the gang members to the Mary River delta in the Northern Territory of Australia.

"You will find the judges here to be most indiscriminate. They don't care how many innocent people that you have beaten, robbed, raped, & killed," continued Malphas.

"That's a relief," said Raymond.

"Is it now?" snorted Malphas as the demons stood by the river with the gang members under their control.

"Where are the judges?" asked Curtis. "I don't see them."

Malphas & his demons lifted each gang member off of their feet, suspending them upside down over the surface of the Mary River.

"Cut them now," commanded Malphas to his demons. Each gang member's throat was cut & their blood flowed into the river. At once the saltwater crocodiles rapidly swam toward the gang members.

The gang members struggled to break free from the grip of the demons, but to no avail.

"I told you that these judges are indiscriminate. They don't see you as thugs, robbers, rapists, or killers. They see you as fresh meat & an easy meal," said Malphas. Malphas & the demons dropped the gang members from above the Mary River just as the massive reptiles ascended from the river depths.

The high-pitched screams & shrieks could be heard from miles around. More blood flowed down the river & when the saltwater crocodiles' feeding frenzy was over, there were no gang member survivors.

The violent gangland activity that had permeated St. Louis decades ago came to an abrupt & sudden stop. Law enforcement on routine patrol found the abandoned cars of both the Bloods & the Crips near St Peters Cemetery just off of St. Louis Avenue. They recovered the bodies of both gang leaders, Dre & Mario. Dre appeared to have a broken neck & Mario appeared to have frozen to death.

"What the hell?" asked Officer Wilson observing both bodies.

"This is some truly weird shit," added Office Browning. "We better call this in..." The

253

police departments of both Wellston & Pine Lawn were called for back-up & investigators from both departments converged on the cemetery combing the area for more clues. Both police departments 911 numbers were overwhelmed with calls from gang family members all making the same claims.

Multiple families were reporting missing persons, strange sightings of dark malevolent specters, & the unnatural lingering burning smell of brimstone. The first couple of reports were taken lightly as the vivid imaginations of drug addicts tripping on some latest high, but as multiple reports began to show consistencies, investigators began to realize that the strange occurrences may have validity. Families pleaded with law enforcement to visit their homes – promising that the safety of the officers & investigators would not be in jeopardy. Investigators did substantiate the presence of the same strange burning odor in multiple homes. They also noted burned sections of the floors of the homes – similar to footprints, but larger than human footprints & shaped differently than human footprints.

"What in God's name are these prints?" wondered one of the investigators. Investigators took photos of the burned foot/paw prints from multiple homes. They tried to collect burnt samples from the various homes to send into Forensics. Official Missing Person alerts were created with family members providing law enforcement with photos of missing loved ones. Missing Person posters with the photos of the missing were posted throughout Wellston, Pine Lawn & the Greater St. Louis Metro area. The Official Missing Persons Reports were also shared with the FBI Field Office in St. Louis. However, no additional leads were

reported for these missing gang members & their family members never saw them again.

Weeks later, an outdoorsman named Trev from Tivendale, Northern Territory, Australia was hiking some distance away from the banks of the Mary River & spotted several patches of clothing strewn about on the ground. It appeared that they were blood-stained & ripped from someone's shirts.

"Poor blokes. Probably got eaten by the crocs," thought Trev. Upon further examination of the patches, he saw two patches with the gang insignia of the Bloods, St. Louis & one patch with the gang insignia of the Crips, St. Louis. Trev quietly & quickly made his way back to his SUV. Trev was unable to find a mailing address to either gang but found an email address for each. Trev took photos of the three patches & upload them to

his computer. He emailed both gangs with the photos & the following message:

All, I'm Trev from Tivendale, Northern Territory, Australia. Today, hiking near the Mary River I found several scraps of clothing near the river bank; two of them had the Bloods insignia, St. Louis & one had the Crips insignia, St. Louis. All three patches appeared to be stained with blood. It appears that members from both gangs may have been victims of crocodiles. The salt-water crocs in the Mary River are plentiful & can grow up to near 20' long. Sorry to be the bearer of bad news, but if they were my mates, I would want to know.
Regards, Trev

In Los Angeles, the Bloods & the Crips called a temporary truce with both gangs reaching out to their counterparts in St. Louis via email. Both gangs got replies back from the families of gang members to learn that all members in St. Louis from both gangs were missing under very disturbing circumstances. They also learned that Dre died of a broken neck & Mario froze to death. In addition, the families shared police photos of the bizarre footprints & police reports of the strange burning smells reported at all of the gang members' homes. The Bloods & the Crips were also sent PDF files of the missing person posters. Families gave them detailed description of the abductions of their respective gang members.

"What the fuck?" asked RayRay - a leader of the Bloods.

"That's some fucked up shit!" exclaimed Rodney – a leader of the Crips.

The electronics for all computers, smartphones, & tablets of both the Bloods & the Crips malfunctioned. All of the screens blacked out & the silhouette of a statue of Satan appeared on all of the screens. Then, they heard a deep, sinister voice come over their electronic devices in an authoritative voice.

"This is Malphas a demon superior. I have some information regarding your missing gang members," suggested Malphas. "Meet me tonight @ midnight downtown Los Angeles. San Julian Park on the corner of 5th street & San Julian St. Besides, I & my legions of demons need to take you on a little trip in time." Malphas let out a dark, sadistic laugh. Then all of his legions of demons also laughed a laugh that made shivers run up & down the spines of the Bloods & the Crips.

"YOU'RE ALL NEXT!" screamed

Malphas. "AND THERE IS NO ESCAPE!"

Chapter 8
Cosa Nostra (Our Thing)

As a member of one of the five Cosa
Nostra families, I had grown up in Bensonhurst,
Brooklyn's most "Italian" neighborhood. My name
is Dominic Salerno or Dom for short. Even though I
grew up in the city, growing up among so many
fellow Italian-Americans sheltered me from some of
the rougher areas of the city. Even so, I learned at
an early age to develop a thick skin. Not only
because of some tough Italian people in the
neighborhood but also because of our connection to
the mob. Respect was not arbitrarily given, it had to
be earned. We were taught from an early age to
never back down, carry yourself with your head
held high, & never dishonor the family. Say what
you mean & mean what you say. Even though
Italian blood runs through my veins, I am proud to

be an American & love my country. My mother sheltered me growing up, so when I graduated high school my father told me that I needed real-world exposure by joining the military. So after serving a stint in the U.S. Army, I was honorably discharged & returned home to Brooklyn as a grown man.

Between the way I grew up & my military training, I thought I was invincible & could handle anything that this life could throw at me. You have to be tough to make it in New York City & I was, but nothing prepared my family & me for the hell that we were about to endure. My family has always been heavily involved in the Roman Catholic Church & despite our connection to Cosa Nostra, we were a family of deep faith & conviction. We were all about to have our faith tested like never before & our family bonds would be pushed to the limit. Before I share the horrors that my family

endured, I can tell you that during my service in the
Army, the troops in my platoon were also a family;
a band of brothers & sisters that was forged in the
heat of battle. If someone had told me ten years ago
that I would have good friends all over America, I
would have told them they were crazy. I always
believed that the only people I cared about lived in
Bensonhurst. As it turns out, fellow soldier Jeff
Redbear from Cherokee, NC turned into one of my
best friends. Even though to us he talked funny, he
had a heart of gold & was fearless.

After months of trying to get Jeff to come
to visit & meet my family, he finally came up in
September of last year. Despite being from the
South, Jeff loved Italian food. So it worked out that
during his visit, we were able to take him to the San
Gennaro Festival in the Little Italy district of
Manhattan. During the festival, Mulberry Street is

transformed into a pedestrian mall on the weekends. All of my family, even my father, liked Jeff because he was honest & brave. Even though I tried to be the overprotective older brother of my sister Elena, I had secretly hoped that Jeff & Elena would hit it off. While Jeff was still visiting us, Elena's senior year of high school had begun & we made plans to go for coffee to talk for a while. Jeff & I waited outside the high school to meet Elena & after the dismissal bell rang, the students made their way out of the school. As Elena was approaching near Jeff's pick-up truck, a dark sedan turned the corner from a side street racing toward us.

As I yelled "LOOK OUT!", gunfire was released & Jeff with his lightning-quick reflexes jumped in front of Elena. Jeff was hit but was alive. The car sped away & no one else was hurt. Frantically, I called 911 & we applied pressure to

Jeff's gunshot wounds until the ambulance arrived.

We were all shaken & gave a statement to the police

with the best description of the car that we could

recall. We followed in Jeff's truck the ambulance

that transported him to the Calko Medical Center on

Bay Parkway in Brooklyn. Elena called our parents

to tell them what happened & to meet us at the

hospital. Although all three bullets were removed,

the surgeons were concerned with internal bleeding.

After surgery, Jeff was in critical condition as one

of three bullets punctured his left lung & he was

moved to a private room where he was in a coma.

My parents met Elena & me in Jeff's hospital room.

We all hugged & my dad went to Jeff's bedside –

looking down at the young man who just became a

hero to our family.

"Mom, Jeff just saved my life," cried

Elena.

Mr. Salerno took Jeff's hand in his & said "Don't die on me kid." A nurse came in to record Jeff's vitals.

"Whatever he needs, give it to him," exclaimed Mr. Salerno. "I'll be paying for all of his expenses here."

"Are you his family?" asked the nurse.

"His family is in North Carolina. We are not his family yet, but if he survives this attack he will be part of our family forever. He just saved our daughter's life," cried Mrs. Salerno. "My son Dom & Jeff served in the Army together & Dom visited Cherokee last year. Dom has notified Jeff's family & they will be here soon."

"We will keep someone with the kid at all times & we will rotate in 4-hour shifts," declared Mr. Salerno. "Dom, you have known him the longest, but we need to let Elena stay first because

of her school tomorrow. You come back later &
relieve her, I will relieve you, & then your mother
will relieve me in the morning. We'll repeat this
until his family arrives."

Mr. Salerno's cell rang & he stepped
away from his family. The call was from Bartolo
Security who served all of the families in Cosa
Nostra.

"Mr. Salerno, this is Vinny with Bartolo
Security. We compiled video footage from the
different street cameras around your daughter's
school. The car is registered to the Lombardo
family in the Commission."

Mr. Salerno burned with anger. "*A fucking
business partner, another family, tried to take out
my baby girl!*" thought Mr. Salerno as he struggled
to keep his composure.

"Would you email me what you got & attach any photos or footage?" asked Mr. Salerno.

"You got it Sir," exclaimed Vinny. "You should receive the email & attachments in the next few moments."

"Grazie Mille (thank you very much) Vinny," said Mr. Salerno.

"Prego (you're welcome) Mr. Salerno," replied Vinny.

Mr. Salerno texted the other family heads "*Mandatory emergency meeting. One Hour. SoHoSoleil, 138 Grand St., Top Floor.*"

An hour later, all the family heads were on the top floor of SoHoSoleil. Mr. Salerno walked around to the Lombardo family head & lunged at him.

"GIVE ME ONE FUCKING REASON WHY I SHOULDN'T SNAP YOUR NECK. HOW

DARE YOU TRY TO PUT A HIT ON MY BABY

GIRL!" screamed Mr. Salerno who had become

completely unglued. The other family heads pulled

Mr. Salerno off of the other man.

"Mr. Salerno, this is not the way the

commission settles disputes between the families,"

said the Head of the Esposito Family. "What proof

do you have?"

Mr. Salerno threw down multiple photos

from various street cameras showing the license

plate of the shooter's car. He also threw down a .pdf

showing the car registered to Triple L Ltd – a

Lombardo business.

"THERE'S YOUR FUCKING PROOF!"

yelled Mr. Salerno.

"Mr. Lombardo, what the hell?" asked Mr.

Esposito.

"Mr. Salerno, Mr. Esposito - our sincere apologies. This car was stolen from the Triple L address early yesterday morning," said Mr. Lombardo. "Mr. Salerno, Vito, how is your daughter?"

"My son's Army buddy saved Elena's life by taking three bullets meant for her," replied Mr. Salerno. "He's in a coma at Calko – fighting for his life."

"Jesus!" cried Mr. Lombardo. "Vito, I'm sorry."

Marko & Bobby stood guard at the elevator & were alerted by Security in the lobby regarding five foreigners urgently pleading to join their meeting.

"Check their IDs & passports," commanded Marko. Moments later, Security replied via walkie talkie radio.

"Sir, they are fathers from Churches in Sicily. They are from Caltanissetta, Catania, Palermo, Ragusa, & Syracuse," replied Main Security.

"Just a moment," replied Marko.

Marko walked to the meeting area & was met by Mr. Esposito.

"What is it Marko?" asked Mr. Esposito.

"Sir, you have down in the lobby five fathers from the Churches of Sicily that desperately need to see you," replied Marko.

"Let them come up Marko," answered Mr. Esposito.

The elevator bell chimed & the five Sicilian fathers made their way to the meeting area.

"Welcome fathers. I am Mr. Esposito," said Mr. Esposito. "What can we do for you?"

"He has returned! The Prince of this world! Satan has come back!" cried the father from the Church in Palermo. "We have come to witness to you what happened in Caltanissetta! We are all in grave danger!" The Father fell to his knees crying & shaking uncontrollably.

"Pull yourself together father," said Mr. Esposito gently patting the father on the shoulder & helped him to stand.

"Why don't you guys have a seat?" requested Vito Salerno. "What happened in Caltanissetta?" Vito offered the fathers something to drink to try to calm them down.

"The Sicilian territorial clan leaders also have a commission as they remain the true head of Cosa Nostra. They were quietly having a clandestine meeting in Caltanissetta at the Antichi Ricordi Hotel & Spa. After their meeting had adjourned, they walked towards Roman Catholic Diocese of Caltanissetta just moments from their hotel," added the father from Palermo. He was still trying to catch his breath, staring down at the floor.

"Keep going father, you're doing good," added Vito. "What happened next?"

"Two priests from the Vatican were requested to come to the Diocese of Caltanissetta to possibly perform an exorcism on a troubled teenage boy who continued to physically harass the citizens," continued the father from Palermo. "The boy claimed that the voices inside him told him to do it. The boy was arrested & placed in solitary confinement to prevent him from harming others or others harming him. Once the priests from the Vatican arrived, they had to determine if an exorcism was warranted. If the exorcism was in fact warranted, the two priests were to both observe &

record the Six Stages of Demonic Possession regarding this boy."

"The Six Stages of Demonic Possession?!?" snorted Mr. Lombardo. "Give me a break! And what are these Six Stages of Demonic Possession?" Lombardo was starting to let his mind wander & he began to feel uneasy about the subject.

"I see, a non-believer," continued the father from Palermo. "The Six Stages of Demonic Possession are Presence, Pretense, Breakpoint, Voice, Clash, & Expulsion. Once the two priests from the Vatican had determined a Presence in the boy, they reported back to Vatican City to get approval to proceed with the exorcism. Once the exorcism was approved, they first had to get the boy transferred from the jail to the basement of the Diocese of Caltanissetta. The boy would not be confined to a jail cell but would be on a hospital bed in the Diocese basement. Both his arms & his legs would be secured with leather straps to minimize the risk of injury to anyone.

"When the exorcism began in the Diocese basement, the Sicilian territorial clan leaders were touring the main floor of the Diocese. They heard the strange, unholy noises coming from the basement unaware that an exorcism was being performed. They were looking to speak to the Bishop of the Diocese, but when they learned that he was away for a time, they decided to go eat & come back later; hoping to see the Bishop before they departed Caltanissetta.

"After they had indulged in authentic Sicilian cuisine, they returned several hours later. The Bishop had yet to return & they continued to hear the same strange noises from the basement. Unable to resist the temptation of witnessing an exorcism & unaware of the dangers, they quietly made their way past Diocese Security into the stairwell of the basement. The stairs of the Diocese basement descended several full flights of stairs – much deeper than the clan leaders had anticipated. They made their way past the scribes' desks, shelves of ancient scrolls & manuscripts, & a map room with ancient maps dating back centuries ago.

"When they neared the closed double-doors, the strange, unholy noises briefly stopped; only to begin again with an ancient tongue being spoken, evil laughter, growls, & howling noises. The clan leaders slowly opened the double-doors, only to find that the two Vatican priests had been decapitated.

"The boy's broken body laid on the floor, broken leather straps still attached to the boy's arms & legs. Both of legs, both of his arms, & his pelvis was broken. With the boy's body broken & no longer of use to the demons, the demons left the boy's body & possessed the Sicilian territorial clan leaders.

"That is why we have come from the Old Country to warn you. The heads of the Sicilian Cosa Nostra are possessed. The families of the clan leaders are in hiding; we suspect that they are being protected in Vatican City, but we are not sure. If the Sicilian Cosa Nostra makes an appearance to you, you must not engage them, but you must directly contact the Brooklyn Diocese's office." The priest wrote down the phone# & gave it to each family boss.

"Now wait just a damn minute," huffed Mr. Lombardo. "How do we know that all of this is true? How do we know that this story is not just a bunch of lies?"

"Because I have seen all of the Security audio/video footage. Everything he told you is true," replied another Sicilian father.

"And who the hell are you?" snorted Mr. Lombardo - clearly disturbed by what he just heard.

"I am Father Genovese, the Bishop of the Roman Catholic Diocese of Caltanissetta," stated Father Genovese.

"Forgive me father for the aggressive line of questioning," replied Mr. Lombardo.

"The clan leaders are now under the control of the demons; making them unpredictable," said Father Genovese. "It is possible that they could target next either you or your families. Have there been any strange occurrences or unexplained occurrences in the last 24 to 36 hours?"

"One of my company cars was stolen yesterday morning. Whoever it was driving it to the high school & tried to kill Vito's daughter Elena

yesterday afternoon," exclaimed Mr. Lombardo.

"They're trying to pit you against one

another – divide & conquer. It's the oldest trick in

the book," replied Father Genovese. "You must not

betray one another now. You must honor your

codes & your alliance. You must have each other's

back – like a band of brothers. You must leave the

city with your families & get them to safety."

"THIS IS MY FUCKING CITY!

THERE'S NO WAY I'M TURNING IT OVER TO

THESE DEMON-POSSESSED WHACKOS!"

yelled Mr. Lombardo.

"Mr. Lombardo, with all due respect, this

is not about you right now; this is about your

family. They are counting on you to get them to

safety & protect them," answered Father Genovese.

"Thank you, Father," replied Vito Salerno.

"Gentlemen, we need to come up with a safe place for our families to hold up until this blows over. Reach out to your contacts to see if they can host us & I'll do the same." Vito texted his wife.

"Hon, change of plans. I need you to ride with Dom to the hospital. Will explain everything there," texted Vito.

"You got it V," replied Donna – Mrs. Salerno. Donna & Dom, Vito's wife & son, met Vito in Jeff's hospital room along with Elena. Vito explained everything to his family while Jeff remained in a coma.

"If Jeff were awake, he may know a place in the Cherokee area," replied Dom. At that moment, there was a knock & the door opened.

"Hi. We're Jeff's parents. Hello Dom."

"I am Lance Redbear & this is my wife Wendy," said Lance.

"Mr. Redbear, I am Vito Salerno, my wife Donna, my daughter Elena, & of course you know my son Dom," said Vito.

"Jeff is our hero, my hero, he saved my life!" cried Elena – wiping the tears from her face.

Wendy approached Jeff's bedside – burying her head in Jeff's pillow with tears in her eyes. "Please come back to us son," whispered Wendy into Jeff's ear.

Vito explained everything to the Redbears & their need to get the families to safety.

"Vito, there's no better place in America to hide out of sight than the mountains of our ancestors. Our Cherokee Reservation is an hour west of Asheville," replied Lance.

"We will be out of sight there?" asked Donna.

"Yes, in the 1800s when the government was trying to resettle all Cherokees from our home in the mountains to Oklahoma, 10,000 of my ancestors hid in mountains & were never rounded up. You'll be safe there, but you'll need to stay off of social media, email & phone to a minimum," answered Lance. "How many family members in all?"

"Around 80 in all. Will you have room for everybody?" asked Vito.

"We got you covered, just let me make a call," replied Lance. "How soon can you book a flight for everyone to Asheville? Once there, my people can get you safely to Cherokee & squared away."

"We have a charter plane that can fly out of the Executive Park Airport nearby @ 8:00am in the morning," said Vito. "Let me give the other families the news."

"All, we have a safe space near the Cherokee Reservation, Western North Carolina. Please be at the Executive Park Airport @ 6:00am. Will fly out by 8:00am to Asheville." texted Vito.

"Okay, we got you guys booked at Wyndham Garden Brooklyn Sunset Park, all meals, room service, & amenities covered as long as you need. Our limo driver, Leo, will take you wherever you need to go. Here's his cell#" exclaimed Donna to Wendy.

Lance got off of the phone.

"Folks, your ground transportation for 80 will be at the Asheville airport at 10:00am," stated Lance. "Thanks for looking after Jeff until we could get here. May the Great Spirit keep you safe in His arms."

After the families hugged, the Salernos left the hospital & went home to pack for their home away from home. The Redbears stayed by Jeff's bedside for another hour, then asked Leo to drive them to their hotel. The next morning, the Cosa Nostra families flew from Brooklyn to Asheville, they were driven from Asheville to Cherokee.

"Oh my God, what a beautiful place," exclaimed Elena. "I understand why the Redbears' ancestors never wanted to leave." Their Cherokee hosts got the families settled in a community of nearby cabins nestled on a secluded mountainside – difficult to see by either air or road.

"It may seem like you're out in the middle of nowhere, but your not. Grocery stores are 15 minutes away & they deliver – so you can remain hidden. There are also some good restaurants nearby, but you may want to lay low until your trouble is over," said Jon River Otter – one of Lance's friends. "If you get cabin fever, there are hiking trails that lead to some amazing waterfalls & lots of wildlife to observe. We can take you to the reservation at night for a tour."

Once the families were settled in, safe & secure, the Cosa Nostra family heads were taken back to Asheville & flew back to New York to defend their territories from the possessed Sicilian Mafia. They met with both the Sicilian fathers & local Catholic leaders at St. Athanasius Church – within walking distance of Calko Medical Center & under the direction of the Catholic Diocese of Brooklyn.

"Once we find these rats that carried out the school attack, we'll take it from there," declared Mr. Lombardo.

"Mr. Lombardo, while we appreciate your assertiveness & bravery, the war we are about to enter cannot be won with weapons of this world. This is a spiritual battle that must be fought by strictly following the Roman Ritual; unfortunately, the two priests from Vatican City did not follow it as closely as they should & it cost them their lives. Before the exorcism was ever started on the Sicilian boy, both medical doctors & psychiatrists ruled out any medical or psychological issues with the boy. Additionally, some of the classic telltale signs of demonic possession were observed in the boy. They included: no appetite, self-inflicted injury to the skin, cold feeling in the room, strange body positions, changes in personality & voice, supernatural strength, & speaking fluent a language that he should not know," replied Father Genovese.

"Our difficulty is we are not just dealing with a single possessed person, but with multiple possessed men as captured by the video in our Diocese. We summoned experienced exorcists from not only New York City, but also from Boston & Philadelphia. The plan is to assign two exorcists for each possessed Sicilian – we think that there are 7 possessed men; based on video footage from Caltanissetta. We have identified the 7 men & have printed their photographs & biographies. The Cosa Nostra in Sicily is represented by city or territory rather than by family affiliation like the U.S. We need you, men, to help us find them – to draw them out in the open, then step back to let us perform the exorcisms," continued Father Genovese as he passed out the profiles of the possessed Sicilians to family heads. "They will probably exhibit similar signs as the teenage boy. They may not be street level; they may be on a rooftop of a skyscraper. Please help us find them with any technology or means at your disposal. May God be with you all."

The family heads departed to do a block-by-block sweep of Brooklyn through surveillance & physical search.

Back at Calko Medical Center a few days later, Jeff came out of his coma to find his parents asleep in chairs by his bedside.

"Mom? Dad?" said Jeff. The Redbears awakened to the sound of Jeff's voice.

"Oh, Jeff! Son! Thank you Great Spirit!" cried Wendy with tears in her eyes. She repeatedly kissed Jeff's face.

"Hello son! Thank you Great Spirit!" exclaimed Lance – hugging his son. There was a knock on the door & they expected hospital staff, but it was another visitor.

"Hey Bro," cried Dom as he went to give Jeff a hug. "Welcome back!"

"Dom? You came back?" asked Lance.

"Yes Sir Mr. Redbear," replied Dom. "I was worried about both my Dad & Jeff, but I am thankful to God that Jeff came out of the coma," Dom told Jeff everything that was going on & Jeff was surprised to learn of the families held up in the mountain cabin community. The doctor had the nurses to test Jeff & track his vital signs for 24 hours, then they released Jeff from the hospital. Donna & Jeff drove back to Cherokee in Jeff's pick-up truck. Lance decided to stay in New York to help Dom & Vito any way that he could.

In Cherokee, there was a knock at the Salerno's cabin. When Elena opened the door, she saw Wendy standing on the porch. They hugged & Wendy told Elena that she had a surprise.

"Elena, there's someone here to see you," said Wendy as the passenger door of her car opened.

"Jeff?!?" replied Elena bounding down the stairs of the cabin. "Oh my God! You're back," giving Jeff a big hug & crying tears of joy. "I was afraid you would die because of me!"

"I didn't want to miss all the fun," replied Jeff. "You know, I love Italian!"

"Italian food or Italian girls?" grinned Elena.

"Most Italian food, but just one Italian girl," replied Jeff giving Elena a kiss on the cheek.

Through air surveillance, the family heads found the possessed Sicilians in a most unlikely location – on top of the Brooklyn Bridge Tower closest to Brooklyn.

"Oh my God! How will we get the exorcists on the tower?" asked Mr. Lombardo.

"We'll get them close to the top of the tower by chopper," replied Mr. Esposito. "The rest of us fellas will go up the old-fashioned way – we'll climb up."

Vito Salerno's cell rang & it was Dom - calling from Lance's hotel. "What's up son?" answered Vito.

"Dad, Jeff came out of the coma. Jeff & Wendy went back to Cherokee," replied Dom.

"Wait, Dom. What do you mean they went to Cherokee? Aren't you there too Dom?" asked Vito.

"No Dad, I came back to Brooklyn to check on Jeff & to help you," answered Dom.

"Dammit son! I didn't want you to come back yet! It's not safe," replied Vito.

"Dad, Mr. Redbear & I just want to help you-" said Dom.

"Listen, son, I love you, but you & Lance have to avoid the Brooklyn Bridge at all costs," interrupted Vito. "You guys gotta get the hell outta here. I love you. Now scram!"

"Wait, dad! Please!" pleaded Dom's phone, but he heard his dad hang up.

"Mr. Redbear, it's happening somewhere on the Brooklyn Bridge," cried Dom with tears in his eyes. "We have to help them."

Each principal exorcist followed the Roman Ritual flawlessly but still struggled to cast out the demons at the top of the Brooklyn Bridge Tower. The Brooklyn Cosa Nostra family heads

raced up the stairs to the top to witness the
exorcisms.

"I command you in the Name of our Lord
& Savior Jesus Christ depart from these sons of
God," commanded the priests as the possessed men
were repeatedly thrown against the tower walls.
"Go back to hell – you slaves of Satan!"

"We won't leave these Sicilian maggots
until we break every bone in their bodies," sneered
the demons.

As the Brooklyn Cosa Nostra family
heads got to the top of the tower, Vito Salerno
called them into a huddle.

"What are you willing to do to save your
family? We say that we love our families, that we're
men of honor, that we're men of faith," exclaimed
Vito. "But what does it all mean if stand idly by &
let our Sicilian brothers suffer such torment? If we

stand idly by until these demon rats come after our wives, our children, & our homes? It's time to make a stand. This ends now!"

The Brooklyn Cosa Nostra family heads walked to the end of the tower, but the priests ran towards them.

"What are you doing? You must not disrupt the exorcisms!" cried the priests.

"Forget about it Father, we got this," replied Vito. Turning toward the possessed men, Vito lit into the demons with a verbal barrage of insults.

"Yo demons. I've met some dumbass son-of-a-bitches in my day, but none as dumb as you idiotic bastards. I mean you guys were angels, right? No mortgage payments, no car payments, no college loans, no working a job you hate. No sickness & no death. All your needs were taken care of. All you had to do was obey God & you had a home in Heaven forever. You guys had it made in the shade, but you went & fucked it up & you wanna blame humans for your stupidity."

The demons stopped tormenting the Sicilian men & started listening.

"What?" they hissed.

"That's right Vito. I mean you wanna talk about the dumbest losers in the history of all Creation, it would be these demons. I mean these demon rats would fuck up a wet dream. It's like the losers at work or school that try to blame others for their own mistakes. I mean, how hard would be to obey God when all of your needs are met? Are you fucking kidding me? Sign me up for that deal seven days a week. Weren't you angels suppose to be smarter than us lowly humans? I mean even we humans would take that deal every time!" continued Mr. Lombardo.

"Uh, Uh," stammered the demons as they became confused & angry.

"Unlike us humans with free will, you damn angels were created sinless & no free will. You were programmed like a fucking computer, but some of you demons malfunctioned & revolted again God. I mean, good God, what did you actually think was going to happen? Did you actually think you could overthrow God, Michael, Raphael, Gabriel & the other archangels? What dope did you snort, smoke, or inject before you made that stupid-ass decision? You fuckers can't plan anything to save your lives. If you were so damn smart you might be able to actually plan, organize, direct, & control your shit, but the only shit yous guys could control is shoveling horse shit on a farm!" added Mr. Esposito.

"TALKING MONKEYS!" screamed the demons as they became angrier.

"Of course, you fucking demons don't know the love of a wife, the love of your children, getting a bonus at work, getting a Christmas gift, or a birthday gift. You want to be like us, but you're not us & you'll never be us! At the end of the day, it sucks to be you! You're all a piss-poor excuse of demons," continued Vito. All of the demons were enraged & let out high-pitched shrieks.

They left the broken bodies of the Sicilians & possessing the bodies of the Brooklyn Cosa Nostra family heads – knocking the men off of the Brooklyn Bridge Tower before the men plunged into the East River. The priests performed the last rites before the men sank into the depths.

"Dad! No! No Dad!" cried Dom as he &
Lance looked on from their car on the bridge. Lance
hugged Dom & held him as Dom cried.

Ambulance helicopters appeared & flew
the injured to the Calko Medical Center. Police
helicopters searched the East River for two hours
but didn't recover any bodies. Several hours later,
witnesses on the river banks pulled in the lifeless
bodies of the Brooklyn Cosa Nostra family heads.

All of the Brooklyn Cosa Nostra families
returned to Brooklyn for the combined funeral of
their husbands, fathers, & friends. Father Genovese,
the Bishop of the Roman Catholic Diocese of
Caltanissetta, presided over the service, with a
number of the priests from St. Athanasius Church
also speaking on behalf of the fallen loved ones.
Dom Salerno gave an impassioned speech praising
the bravery & sacrifice of each man to protect his

respective family. Lance Redbear gave an inspirational speech offering the hope that each family would someday see their fallen loved ones again. Memorial plaques were installed at both the Brooklyn Bridge & St. Athanasius Church in Brooklyn praising their selfless acts & for making the ultimate sacrifice for their families.

Father Genovese visited the Sicilian territorial clan leaders recovering in Calko Medical Center. The Sicilians had very little memory of what had transpired; Father Genovese explained to them all the ultimate sacrifice made by the Brooklyn Cosa Nostra family heads.

After the Sicilians recovered & returned to Sicily, the Sicilian territorial clan leaders unanimously voted to erect a memorial statute in Caltanissetta with the names of the Brooklyn Cosa Nostra family heads who died to save them. They also decided to send one million dollars to each surviving family in memory of their lost loved ones.

The Salernos returned to Brooklyn, New York, but not before Jeff took Elena to the top of Mingo Falls on the Cherokee Reservation & proposed. The following spring, Elena graduated from high school in Brooklyn. Weeks later, Jeff & Elena were married in Brooklyn before making their home in Cherokee. Donna partnered with expert craftsmen in Cherokee & opened on Mulberry Street The Cherokee Creations Jewelry Store. Next door to his mom, Dom opened Vito's Italian Restaurant named after his father.

As time went on, the families picked up the pieces & supported each other through their darkest days. Even amid their tears, they never forgot their fallen loved ones & the legacy of bravery, sacrifice, & love that they left behind.

Chapter 9
Realm of the Jinns

A jinn can live for thousands of years. He or she is dual dimensional with the ability to exist & operate in both the visible & the invisible realms. They determine whether or not if we can see them transitioning between the two realms at will; we see them only if they want us to see them. Over a billion Muslims around the world believe in the jinn. Arabs believed in the jinn long before Islam was introduced. Its existence is believed in many countries & cultures around the world – albeit in different variations. The Jinns are created from fire. Unlike demons, Jinns were not cast out of Heaven for rebelling against God. Like humans, they were created neither as believers or non-believers. They can follow Islam, Judaism, Christianity, or be non-believers. According to believers familiar with

Jinns, it is only the non-believing Jinns that seek to harm humans; the believers pose no danger to humans. They leave us alone.

Like humans, Jinns have no use for demons; this is particularly accurate for the believing Jinns who want to go to Heaven. Rebellious angels cast out of Heaven only to become demons are probably not the best examples for Jinns to follow. Therefore, Jinns really have nothing to discuss with demons; Jinns did not cause the angels to fall nor did human beings. Jinns have more in common with humans than they do with demons. They consider demons a lost cause because the fools did it to themselves. Jinns consider demons to be the ultimate underachievers in the history of Creation. Where the Jinns gather, there is no room for foolish demons. Demons cannot threaten the Jinns with being cast into a lake of fire

– again the Jinns were made from fire & they would

not be intimidated by such a pointless threat.

Demons that appear in the realm of the jinns are

issued a stern warning – stay away or suffer the

consequences.

As is the case of Munku Sardyk, the snow-

capped mountain range that separates Russia from

Mongolia. The mountain range rises 11,500 feet &

has some very rugged, harsh terrain. 2,500 years

ago, a demon aimlessly wandered into a cave that

had long been claimed by the Jinns. This cave was

just below the summit of the highest mountain in

Munku Sardyk & was virtually inaccessible to most

humans. As a result of the demon's intrusion into

the realm of the Jinns, a warning sign had been

raised at the entrance of this cave in multiple

languages to make their warning more prominent.

These were the most common & oldest languages
used in this region of the world:

(Russian) - Демоны не допускаются!

(Mongolian) - Ямар ч чөтгөрийг
зөвшөөрөөгүй!

(Chinese) - 禁止惡魔！

(Kazakh) - Жындарға тыйым салынады!

(Ukrainian) - Не дозволено демонів!

(Hebrew) - אסור לשדים!

(Arabic) - لا الشياطين المسموح بها!

(Lithuanian) - Neleidžiama jokių demonų!

This warning sign, translated in English,
simply warned "No Demons Allowed!" Like
humans, jinns do not always see eye to eye, but one
thing that they all agree on is their disdain for
demons. Both believing & non-believing jinns loath

demons & will put aside their differences when it comes to dealing with demons. They will coordinate attacks to severely punish an intruding demon. While they typically do not kill demons, they can inflict such a great deal of pain to a demon that the demon simply finds somewhere else to dwell.

2,500 years ago, the Jinns had previously warded off the Slavic demon Chort from their cave & had not seen him since, but 50 years ago the Jinns had set booby traps for Chort's eventual return. As Chort had the distinct smell of brimstone (Sulphur), the Jinns had learned from human Chemistry teachings certain chemicals that reacted to Sulphur – all meant to terrorize any unsuspecting demon. The traps were located at the far end of the tunnel to be sprung *after* the demons fled from the Jinns. Chort did return & ignored the warning sign.

As Chort descended deeper & deeper into the cave he heard voices but saw no one. Chort heard the sudden rush of something approaching & he was violently thrown against the craggy walls of the tunnel. Chort screamed in pain & was repeatedly picked up & slammed against the tunnel walls.

"WE TOLD YOU TO NEVER COME BACK TO OUR CAVE, BUT YOU IGNORED US!" screamed an invisible evil jinn. By now, Chort was writhing in pain.

"GET OUT NOW, YOU SATANIC PIECE OF SHIT," yelled the evil jinn. "GO BACK TO HELL WHERE YOU BELONG!"

Chort ran further into the cave & heard another sudden rush; looking towards the sound, he heard nothing but felt holy water splash against his face – which intensely burned him across his face as he whimpered in pain.

"I follow the Roman Catholic faith, Our Lord Jesus & the Virgin Mary. You were just splashed with blessed Holy water from the Gave de Pau River near Lourdes, France!" replied an invisible jinn. Chort ran further into the cave & he heard the sounds of something approaching from both his left & his right.

"This is the Star of David," said a visible jinn pressing it against the left side of Chort's face – scarring his face as Chort screamed in agony. "I follow God the Father of Abraham, Issac, & Jacob!"

"This is the Crucifix," stated a 2nd visible jinn pressing it against the forehead of Chort's face – burning his face as flames ignited once the cross touched him as he screamed in excruciating pain.

"The Cross of our Lord & Savior Jesus Christ! Depart from our cave at once!"

Chort now heard the Arabic recital of the Holy Quran & he burned intensely throughout his body as the Jinns commanded him to get out now.

As Chort ran toward the light at the far end of the tunnel, he was hit with pressured air reacting with the Sulphur on his skin. Fluorine was sprayed on his skin from booby traps as Chort trembled in pain. Molten Sulphur dripped on him from above making him smell even worse. He had to run over hot aqueous potassium hydroxide which also reacted with the remaining Sulphur on his skin as by now he was thoroughly terrified. Running out of the tunnel, Chort heard the laughter of the Jinns.

"Don't ever come back, you Satanic maggot," warned the Jinns and Chort never returned to their cave.

Chapter 10
The Greatest Regret

Michael, the warrior archangel, gazed upon the vast Army of Heaven of over 100,000,000 strong with a heavy heart & a flood of memories of how Heaven used to be before the creation of humans. He was very obedient & very humble. Michael always knew that this day would come & yet it was still a shock to his system.

"This is really happening," thought Michael.

He did not always hate Satan or the demons, but more than anything he was angry at them. Angry for them rebelling against God & Heaven. Angry at them for all of the human suffering, death & destruction that they caused. Angry for all of the human souls that were led astray & the subsequent sadness that it caused God.

Angry that all of the angels were not together in Heaven. It was not supposed to be this way.

Both Heaven & Earth were in disarray because of Satan & his demons. Heaven should have never had a rebellion – all of the angels should be serving God together & enjoying the fellowship of the Heavenly hosts. Earth should have remained a Paradise for humankind & their existence should have never been contaminated by evil.

"Curse you brother! Curse you for all of the pain & suffering you have caused us all!" murmured Michael. One of his subordinates walked up beside him.

"Sir, what did you say?" said the subordinate.

"Never mind," replied Michael. "We need to move when He gives us the word to go. Is everyone prepared?"

"Yes, Sir! We have the full Army on standby," answered the subordinate.

As many times as Satan & his demons perverted the Scriptures when trying to deceive humans, they all knew what the Scriptures really said & it was a source of absolute terror for them. They knew the fate that awaited them. Although they knew the signs indicated that judgment would come soon, neither angels nor demons knew when God will give the command to Michael to bring their punishment. Up until now, the demons had tried to put their fate in the back of their minds, but now came their moment of truth.

In hell, the demons were now beginning to stare at Satan with contempt & disgust. The murmuring & complaining had begun to take a toll on all of them. As their impending doom drew near, the demons' motivation to deceive any more humans was gone. They had all come face to face with a harsh dose of reality & they were beginning to comprehend how it could have all gone so wrong.

"We hate to admit it, but they were right," commented Legion to Belial, Malphas, & Mangum.

"Right about what?" snorted Belial – clearly in a very foul mood.

"The humans who sacrificed themselves on the Brooklyn Bridge when we drowned them in the river.

"They said & I quote 'All your needs were taken care of. All you had to do was obey God & you had a home in Heaven forever. You guys had it made in the shade, but you went & fucked it up. Now you wanna blame humans for your stupidity.' We did have all of the needs met & as much as we hate humans, we did do it to ourselves.

"They also questioned what we actually thought would happen by defying God. They also said that it was a stupid-ass decision & that we didn't know how to plan anything," observed Legion.

"THEY'RE JUST FUCKING TALKING MONKEYS! WHAT THE HELL DO THEY KNOW?" replied Belial.

"We underestimated them. We tried to divide by ethnicity, race, religion, gender, class, & any other divisive characteristic. Sure, some of them were deceived & led astray, but some of them withstood the best onslaught that we could muster & yet they still remained faithful to God," said Mangum. "They will spend eternity in Heaven & we will not."

"THEY HAVE NEVER COMPARED TO US & THEY NEVER WILL!" screamed Belial.

"It doesn't matter now. Look at how many times we tried to wipe them out. Plagues, famines, natural disasters, & yet they lived. Genghis Khan, Nero, Judas Iscariot, Vlad Dracula, Hitler, Stalin, Hirohito, Mao Zedong, Osama bin Laden, & Saddam Hussein abused, enslaved, killed, raped, & tortured millions of them – yet so many of them remained faithful to God. We used every single temptation to deceive them, yet so many of them remained faithful & true. Can we say the same thing of ourselves?" asked Malphas.

"THEY DON'T DESERVE HEAVEN! THEY DON'T DESERVE TO LIVE! THEY SHOULD HAVE NEVER BEEN CREATED! I HATE ALL HUMANS!" yelled Belial.

"Feel free to continue you with your little temper tantrum, but you don't get to decide who goes to Heaven & who doesn't," replied Mangum.

Belial retreated away from the other demons & sulked.

Mangum & Malphas approached Satan & threw him down to the ground.

"This is all your fault," said Mangum. "Did you stop to think for a millisecond if defying God was the best idea?"

"Why didn't you plan your little coup better? What the hell made you think that you could defeat God & the archangels? You have got to be the dumbest motherfucker in the history of Creation," added Malphas. "My greatest regret is listening to the stupidest son-of-a-bitch that ever lived. Let me spell it out for you – that would be you" as he punched the left side of Satan's face as hard as he could.

"I couldn't agree more," said Mangum as he kicked Satan in the groin multiple times. "Stay the hell away from us or we will all jump your ass & you will be begging to be thrown in the lake of burning sulfur. You damn dickhead!" Satan crawled away from everyone & hid behind some boulders – now afraid of being jumped by the other demons.

Michael received the sign from God to proceed & he directed the trumpeters to sound the trumpet to begin the attack on hell. Millions of angels overpowered the demons – casting them into the lake of fire. A chorus of high-pitched shrieks, screams, & crying ensued. There was indeed weeping & gnashing of teeth. The only remaining demons were Satan, Belial, & Legion.

"EAT SHIT & DIE SONS OF GOD!" yelled Legion.

"You first," replied four angels who cast Legion into the lake of burning fire. Multiple voices

coming from Legion screamed in intense pain &
suffering.

"GO TO HELL YOU TRAITORS OF
ANGELS!" yelled Belial as a group of angels
through him into the lake of burning fire. Belial
hissed, shrieked, & moaned as he endured the
scorching pain.

"News flash Belial – we're already here to
destroy you," replied Gabriel. "But don't worry, we
won't be staying long. We have a little party to
attend in Heaven while you are getting your nuts
barbequed!"

Satan now stood alone against the Army
of Heaven.

"Am I glad to see you guys! Thanks for
coming to rescue me!" exclaimed Satan.

"Rescue you? That's not going to happen," replied Raphael. Satan ran towards Michael.

"Michael! Michael! Michael! You're the big guy. What do you say – can you give me a head start?" requested Satan. Michael shook his head.

"You have been God's biggest disappointment. He had such big plans for you – before you decided to defy him; before you decided to disobey him. Not only did you disobey him, but you also deceived some of our brothers to follow you in the rebellion. Even now, you fail to take responsibility for your own actions. You really didn't think things through before you decided to try your little coup, did you? You made decisions based on emotions instead of making decisions based on logic," replied Michael.

"Someone had to stand up for us angels against the talking monkeys that replaced us in the eyes of God. Someone had to call out the injustice & the blatant disregard of us angels. I just pointed out some inconsistencies in Management that needed to be addressed," answered Satan – desperately looking around for an escape.

"That was not your decision to make. You knew the rules; we were there at the beginning of Creation when they were first written," replied Michael. "You just thought you knew better than God."

"I DID KNOW BETTER THAN GOD! HE REPLACED US WITH THOSE DAMN FUCKING TALKING MONKEYS WHO TURNED THEIR BACKS ON HIM TIME & AGAIN!" yelled Satan.

"You deceived them Satan," answered Michael.

"I did what I could in the allotted time that I had – me & my former associates!" exclaimed Satan as he let out a nervous laugh.

"Time's up. Throw him in the lake of burning sulfur," commanded Michael. Four archangels picked up Satan who was struggling to break free.

"NO! NO! NO!" screamed Satan as he was thrown into the lake of burning sulfur. He screamed in absolute agony, shrieking at the top of his lungs, & crying bitterly.

Michael & his Army returned to Heaven. Michael, Raphael, Gabriel, & the other archangels drafted & signed the final report attesting to all that they had witnessed in hell regarding the enforcement of a final judgment on Satan & his demons. After they adjourned from this solemn

meeting, they joined in a most elegant & inviting

banquet to celebrate their victory.

Made in the USA
Middletown, DE
23 October 2020